THE GREAT
SOCKATHON

THE GREAT
Sockathon

Michael Delaney

Dutton Children's Books

New York

Copyright © 2004 by Michael Delaney

CIP Data is available.

Published in the United States by Dutton Children's Books,
a division of Penguin Young Readers Group
345 Hudson Street, New York, New York 10014
www.penguin.com
Designed by Richard Amari
Printed in USA • First Edition
2 4 6 8 10 9 7 5 3 1
ISBN 0-525-46856-0

For my mom and dad and
for Ned, Sue, Molly, and John
M.D.

THE GREAT
SOCKATHON

SEPTEMBER 24, 1932

1 Ginny

IT all happened so quickly, so unexpectedly. Yet that's all it takes sometimes: a moment. One unforgiving, unlucky moment.

We were at the village green, Eliza and I, climbing up the old balm of Gilead tree. I was about halfway up the tree when I stopped, unable to climb another inch higher. Eliza, meanwhile, bounded up the tree as swiftly as a monkey. Unlike me, Eliza had no fear of heights. Eliza feared nothing.

"Jeepers!" cried Eliza from way up high in the tree.

"What?" I asked as I held on tightly to the branch I was sitting on.

"Ginny, you've got to see this view!" said Eliza. "I can see all the way to Long Island!"

"You can?" From where I sat, I couldn't see anything through the thick leaves.

We had skipped school to come to the village green. It was Eliza's idea to skip school. She wanted to see Franklin Roosevelt, the governor of New York. He was running for president against the Republican, Herbert Hoover. With only about a month left before the general election, Roosevelt was traveling around the country, campaigning. Today, he had come to the village green in New Elder, Connecticut, to give a speech at the gazebo.

It was also Eliza's idea to climb up the balm of Gilead tree. There were so many people crowded about the gazebo, she thought we'd be able to see better up in the tree.

I didn't want to climb the tree. It made me uneasy. It seemed wrong somehow, like climbing on the statue of the Civil War soldier that was also on the village green. After all, the tree was over two hundred years old. It had been around during George Washington's time. Legend had it that Washington once slept under the tree. He was in a horse-drawn carriage on his way to Boston when, passing through the village, he saw the shady balm of Gilead tree growing on the village green. Weary from traveling, hot from the midday sun, Washington ordered his driver to stop. He climbed out and took a nap in the tree's generous shade.

"I really don't think we should be doing this, Eliza," I said.

"Doing what?"

"Climbing Old Balmy." That was the balm of Gilead tree's nickname.

"Why not?" she asked.

"Well, for one thing, it could us get into trouble."

"Oh, don't be such an old lady!" said Eliza.

"I'm not an old lady," I protested.

"Well, you certainly sound like one."

"Well, I'm not."

"Come on, Ginny, you don't want to miss out on seeing Franklin Roosevelt, do you?"

"No," I admitted.

"Well, then, get yourself up here."

I tilted my head back. Through a gap in the leaves, I could see Eliza perched on a branch, gazing down at me. She smiled, waved.

"I can see fine from here," I said.

"Oh, you cannot!"

I tried to let go of the branch I was clinging to and grab the branch above me, but I couldn't.

"I can't," I confessed.

"Of course you can!" replied Eliza. The word *can't* was not in Eliza's vocabulary. "Just don't look down."

"Believe me," I said, "I have no intention of looking down."

The next thing I knew, Eliza had scrambled down to the branch that was above my head. Leaning over, she held out her hand.

"Here, give me your hand," she commanded.

"Eliza, really, I'm fine just where I am."

"You can do it, Ginny," insisted Eliza. "Just give me your hand."

Slowly, reluctantly, I let go of my branch. As I started to reach for Eliza's outstretched hand, I heard the most terrifying sound.

Craaaaaaaaaack!

I shrieked and grabbed hold of my branch. I held on for dear life. I thought for sure that the branch I was sitting on had snapped and I was about to plunge to my death.

But I was wrong. It wasn't my branch.

It was Eliza's.

SUMMER, 2003

2 Sabrina

I HAD heard that the old balm of Gilead tree on the village green was haunted. Everyone had heard *that*. In New Elder, the town I live in, the balm of Gilead—or Old Balmy, as some people called the tree—was as famous as the Loch Ness monster. Maybe even *more* famous. But while everyone might have heard about strange and unexplainable incidents—a patch of leaves shaped like a skull mysteriously turning a bright, fiery red in the middle of May, eerie moaning late at night—I didn't know of a single person who had actually witnessed a real, live ghost.

Not that people didn't try. Every Halloween, it seemed, the local TV station sent a reporter to the balm of Gilead tree. The reporter would stand under the tree and talk about the ghost as if it were a groundhog on Groundhog Day.

"Will this be the night that the ghost comes out?" the reporter, holding a microphone up to his or her mouth, would ask. It never was.

I always thought it would be fun if my friends—Megan, Connie, and Daisy—and I hid behind the tree during one of these broadcasts and made spooky ghost sounds. But we never did.

As I say, the ghost was just local lore. So far as I knew, nobody had ever witnessed a ghost at the balm of Gilead tree. All that changed, however, one hot, muggy evening in June when a girl in town heard one.

That girl was *me*.

3 Megan

SABRINA swears she heard a ghost that evening on the village green. She's 100 percent sure of it. But whenever we talk about it, I always ask the same question: Why didn't I hear it?

I mean, hey, I was at the gazebo, too, that evening. In fact, I was even closer to the balm of Gilead tree than Sabrina. It seems to me if a ghost said something, I would have heard it, too.

But I didn't.

And it's not like I wasn't paying attention, either. That's something Mr. Eldridge, my fifth-grade teacher, marked on my last report card. He said I don't pay enough attention in class. Well, I do! Ask me anything about that evening. I'll tell you exactly what happened.

Want to know what the weather was like? It sucked. The entire day was overcast, drizzly, and steamy hot. Not sunny and smelling of sunscreen and coconut tanning oil the way the first day of summer vacation is supposed to.

I was with Mom in our Jeep Grand Cherokee. We were on Route 1, on our way back from seeing Great-aunt Carrie.

Great-aunt Carrie was Mom's great-aunt, not mine. She was ninety-six years old and lived in the Chatham Green Nursing Home.

I can even tell you what we were listening to on the car radio: WBAZ-FM—the station that plays the best hits of the sixties, seventies, and eighties. Mom works at WBAZ-FM. A DJ who calls himself Boom-boom Brogan was on the air. He played a song about how, if you're going to San Francisco, you should be sure to wear flowers in your hair. Then he played a song about some guy who left a cake out in the rain. Talk about weird!

Then Boom-boom Brogan said, "Fasten your seat belts, Boomers: it's time for a blast from the past! Yes, it's time to travel back in the rock 'n' roll time machine!"

Mom, who worked in the radio station's marketing department, reached over and turned up the volume. The rock 'n' roll time-machine promotion had been her idea.

"I'm setting the dial to the summer of 1969, the year of the big Woodstock rock festival," said Boom-boom Brogan. "Oops, I forgot to close the time-machine door." What sounded like a heavy, creaky vault door closed with a solid thud. Then there was a loud *swooosh!* sound. This was followed by a burst of wild applause, cheers, the strum of an electric guitar.

"Hey, groovy, I'm at Woodstock!" Boom-boom Brogan cried excitedly. Just then, loud thunder grumbled from the radio. "Rats, it's raining!" he said. "Wouldn't you know it? I left my umbrella in the twenty-first century!"

I rolled my eyes and said, "Yuk! Yuk!" Mom smiled—or

sort of smiled. She looked tired. I could tell she'd had a long day.

"Let's get a pizza to take home," she said.

"Sure," I replied.

Mom ordered it on her cell phone while we were stopped at a traffic light. She only had to order for the two of us. My parents are divorced.

We got off Route 1 and drove into the business section of New Elder. Mom drove down Elm Street and pulled into a parking spot on the side of the village green near the pizza parlor. We both got out.

"Isn't that Sabrina?" Mom asked as we were about to go into Mr. Pizza. Mom was peering in the direction of the village green.

I turned to look. A slim girl with shoulder-length blond hair tied back in a ponytail was sitting on the steps of the gazebo. A mountain bike lay on the grass just a few yards away.

"Yeah, it is," I said. I couldn't figure out what she was doing there. She didn't seem to be doing much of anything, just hanging out. "I'll be right back," I told Mom.

When Sabrina saw me coming, she smiled and waved.

"Hey, girl!" she said. "What are you doing here?"

"Getting a pizza with my mom," I said. "What are *you* doing here?"

Sabrina groaned. "I had a fight with my mother."

I should've guessed. Sabrina and her mother were constantly having fights.

"What about?" I asked.

"Books," replied Sabrina. "My mother gave me a list of books she wants me to read over the summer."

That sounded like Sabrina's mother, all right. Mrs. Ingalls was a very hands-on mother, a real control freak. "You're kidding me!" I told her. "It's the first day of vacation!"

Sabrina was about to say something when, suddenly, a strange look came across her face.

"Who was that?" she asked, wide-eyed, staring at me.

"Who was who?" I glanced around. We were the only two people on the village green.

"I thought I heard a girl's voice," Sabrina said.

"I didn't hear anyone."

"Oh, come on, Meggy, you must've heard her!"

"Where'd the voice come from?" I asked.

"It came from . . ." Sabrina's voice trailed off. "From the balm of Gilead tree!"

"Get out of here!" I told her.

"It did!"

I turned and looked at the huge old balm of Gilead tree. It was almost dusk and a few fireflies were flying about, flickering on and off, near the massive, dark gray trunk. When I was six years old, Mrs. Bedikian, my first-grade teacher, took our class on a field trip to see the tree. She had us circle the tree and hold hands. It took fourteen kids with their arms stretched as far as we could stretch them to embrace the tree. I have a picture of it. You can pick me out real easy—I'm the only African-American in the photograph.

"Ha! Ha! Very funny!" I said. "I should have known this was a joke."

"I'm not kidding!"

I have to say, Sabrina did look pretty serious. Sabrina loves to kid around. She always smiles, though, and gives herself away. But she wasn't smiling now.

"There it is again!" cried Sabrina. "It's a girl's voice. Listen!"

I listened. I heard a bird twittering and a truck grinding its gears over on Main Street, but that's all.

Sabrina sprang to her feet and ran over to the tree. "Who's up there?" she called as she peered upward. "Who's there?"

I came over and stood beside Sabrina. "Sabrina, you're freaking me out! Now stop it!"

Sabrina paid no attention. "Who's up there?" she called again.

I looked up at the mass of snaking branches and millions of green leaves. There was no one in the tree.

Suddenly, Sabrina let out a loud, startled gasp. She put her hand to her mouth, staring at me. She looked scared out of her wits.

"What is it?" I asked. "What's the matter?"

"She—she—"

"She what?" I said.

"She said . . . 'Help me.'"

"*Help me?*"

"That's not all, Meggy! She said our names! She knows who we are!"

4 Connie

I WAS on the Internet when Sabrina called. I was doing a Google search on Guilin, China. That's where my baby sister is. Well, she isn't my baby sister yet. But she will be at the end of the year if all goes well. My parents are going to adopt a baby girl. That'll make two girls they got from an orphanage in China. The first girl? Me.

When Sabrina called, she didn't come right out and say, "Hey, Connie, guess what just happened?" That's what *I* would have done if it had been me. But not Sabrina. She beat around the bush.

"Tell me about ghosts," she said.

"What do you want to know?" I asked. She knew that I knew a lot about ghosts. I'm a ghost fanatic. I love ghost stories. The creepier, the better.

"Is it possible to hear a ghost without actually seeing one?"

"Sure it is."

"Can one person hear a ghost but not another?"

"Of course," I replied.

"Even if the person is standing right next to you?"

"It happens all the time," I replied. "You need to see more ghost movies, Sabrina. Why are you asking me this, anyway?"

There was a pause on the other end. Then Sabrina said, "I heard a ghost tonight, Connie." She said it in a quiet voice. Like she was afraid she might be overheard.

"You *what?*" I cried, startled.

"I . . . I heard a ghost."

"What are you talking about? Are you sure? When? *Where?*"

"At the balm of Gilead tree."

I felt my spine tingle. "Tell me more!"

"Well, we were at the gazebo and—"

"*We?* Who's *we?*"

"Megan and I."

"What were you doing?"

"Nothing. Just hanging out."

"What time was this?"

"I don't know. About eight-thirty or so."

"So what happened?"

"Well, Megan and I were at the gazebo, just talking, when I heard this girl's voice. It was so creepy, Connie! The weird thing is, Megan didn't hear anything."

"Nothing?"

"No. She thinks it was just my imagination."

"Do you think you imagined it?"

"No, I don't. I heard a girl's voice. I'm positive I did."

"What did she say?"

"She said, 'Help me.'"

"*Help me?* Why would she say that?"

"I don't know," said Sabrina. "She also spoke our names."

"Whose names?"

"Mine and Megan's."

"No way!" I cried.

"I swear!"

"How could she know your names?"

"That's what I was hoping you could tell me," said Sabrina. "You're the ghost expert."

I had no answer, though. Not a clue. So far as I knew, the only way a ghost would know your name was if he or she knew you in life, before the person became a ghost.

Then Sabrina said, "I haven't told anyone about this. Only you. Well, you and Megan. Do you think I should tell someone?"

"Tell them what?" I asked. "That a ghost spoke to you? I doubt anyone would believe you. They might even laugh."

"So what should we do?"

"We need to find out more about this ghost," I said. "We need to find out who she was in life."

"I'll call a meeting," said Sabrina.

We said good-bye and hung up. I just sat there for a few moments, thinking about what Sabrina had said, trying to make sense of it. But I couldn't. How could a ghost know Sabrina's and Megan's names?

As I sat there, a new message came in. From Sabrina. She

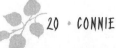

had just sent it. She had also sent the e-mail to Megan Geherty and Daisy Deitz. It was titled "ghost" and said:

meeting tomorrow. 9 am. my house.
c u then. sabrina :)

5 Daisy

I COULDN'T believe Sabrina had told Connie about the ghost before she told me. I didn't mind her telling Megan, though. After all, Megan was right there at the gazebo when Sabrina heard the ghost. But *Connie?* What was with *that?* I mean, *I'm* Sabrina's oldest friend! We've known each other since preschool. Sabrina and I have done nearly everything together. Soccer. Swimming lessons at the YWCA. Ballet classes. Piano lessons. Day camp. Why, we're practically sisters! That's why I was so mad when I found out that she had told Connie about the ghost before me. I didn't hear what happened at the balm of Gilead until the next morning, when the four of us were in Sabrina's kitchen, sitting around the table.

I was the *last* to know!

"So what's this about a ghost?" I asked. After I had seen Sabrina's "ghost" message," I e-mailed back, asking her to tell me more. She hadn't responded, though. I also tried to call, but I only got the Ingalls' voice mail. "How come you didn't e-mail me back, Sabrina? Or call? This isn't another one of your jokes, is it? So what's this about?"

"I heard a ghost at the balm of Gilead tree," replied Sabrina.

"No way! Really? You serious? Awesome!"

Megan rolled her eyes at me. I guess she thought I was overreacting. "Listen," she said. "I was right there at the gazebo, too, and *I* didn't hear a thing."

"Connie says it's not unusual for a ghost to speak to one person and not another," said Sabrina.

I turned and looked at Connie. Of the four of us, she was the smallest and quietest. She was so unlike me. I was the biggest and loudest. Connie was also the smartest. Connie was so smart, she was in the advanced learning program at school.

"*You* know about this?" I asked.

"Sabrina called me last night," said Connie.

"You did?" I said, surprised, turning to Sabrina.

"Oh, sure," said Megan, "maybe in movies, ghosts exist, but, hey, this is real life."

"Thanks for calling me," I said to Sabrina.

I think Sabrina felt kind of bad that she hadn't called me, because she retold the whole story, right from the very beginning, even though Megan and Connie had already heard it.

"She knew your *names?*" I blurted out when Sabrina got to that part of the story.

"That's what I can't figure out," said Connie. "How could a ghost know your names? There's only one thing I can think of. She must be able to leave the tree and spy on us."

"*Spy* on us?" said Megan, widening her eyes.

"Can a ghost *do* that?" Sabrina asked Connie.

"Okay, time out!" I said, making a time-out "T" sign with my hands. "Listen, before we all start freaking out, can I ask a couple of questions?" I looked at Sabrina. "When you were at the tree last night, did you say Megan's name?"

Sabrina thought for a moment. "I don't remember. I'm sure I did, though."

I turned to Megan. "Did you say Sabrina's name?"

"Probably."

"There's our answer!" I said. "The ghost heard you say each other's names."

"You know, I bet Daisy's right," said Sabrina. She looked at Megan. "The ghost called you Meggy. I'm the only one who ever calls you that."

"Well, I guess that explains how the ghost knew your names," said Connie. She sounded kind of mad. I think she was annoyed that I had figured it out and not her.

"We still don't know why she asked for help," said Sabrina.

"Maybe she was murdered!" I said. "Maybe she wants *us* to find her killer! Maybe she can't rest until we bring her killer to justice!"

"It's true ghosts can't rest if they have unfinished business they need to take care of," said Connie.

"You mean, it's true according to the movies," said Megan.

"We need to learn more about this ghost," said Sabrina.

"How do we do that?" I asked. I got up to see if the Ingalls had anything good to eat in their breadbox. They did:

a box of powdered-sugar doughnuts. "Hey, anybody want a doughnut?" I asked, helping myself to one.

"Since when did this become your house, Daisy?" asked Megan.

"It's fine," said Sabrina. "Really. So back to the subject. How can we find out more about this ghost?"

"The library might have something," suggested Connie.

"The library?" said Sabrina.

"It might," said Connie. "I don't know for sure. I mean, it *is* just a legend."

"There's only one way to find out," said Sabrina.

"Let's go!" I said.

"I'll meet you guys there," Connie said. "I have to do my paper route first."

Connie had just gotten a newspaper route. She delivered *The New Elder Times*—our area's local newspaper. It was her summer job.

"Can't you do it later?" asked Sabrina.

Connie shook her head. "It's supposed to be delivered in the morning. Besides, Mrs. Campbell will call and complain about me if she doesn't get her newspaper ASAP."

"Who's Mrs. Campbell?" I asked.

"One of the people I deliver newspapers to."

"Tell you what," said Sabrina. "We'll all help you. Then we'll go to the library."

We started to get up from the table.

"Wait!" said Sabrina. "Before we go, let's all promise not to tell anyone else about the ghost. We don't want people making fun of us."

We reached out our hands, hooked our pinkies, and made a pinkie promise.

Connie lived just down the street from Sabrina. It was a shady tree-lined street with old Victorian houses. When we got to Connie's house, two bundles of newspapers were lying on her asphalt driveway. The newspaper delivery truck had left them there.

Connie went into her garage and came back with a pair of scissors and a little, rickety-looking, two-wheel shopping cart. She snipped the rope that was wrapped around one of the newspaper bundles. She let out a loud gasp.

"Oh, my gosh!" she cried. "Guys, look at this!"

Connie held up the newspaper. On the front page was a big color photograph of the balm of Gilead tree. Beside it was an article with a headline in large type that said:

275-Year-Old Tree to Get the Ax

6 Sabrina

THEY'RE cutting down Old Balmy?" cried Daisy. She sounded shocked.

I couldn't believe it, either. "Why are they doing that?" I asked.

"The town hired a tree company to inspect it," said Connie as she skimmed the article. "They discovered the tree is all rotten inside."

"But they can't cut it down!" I said. "That tree is two hundred and seventy-five years old! George Washington slept under it!"

Connie read aloud: "'In a telephone interview, Mayor Nancy Sargent said she and members of the town board discussed the possibility of buying a brace for the tree, but it was decided that it just wasn't feasible.'"

"What does 'feasible' mean?" asked Daisy.

"It means doable," I said.

"Actually, Sabrina, it means practical," said Connie.

"Practical, doable, same thing," I said. Then I asked, "Does it say why it wasn't feasible?"

"It would cost too much money," said Connie.

"How much is too much?" I asked.

"Try six thousand dollars."

"That's not that much."

Megan looked at me like I was out of my mind.

"Well, not for a town," I said.

"The mayor says the tree is just going to keep on rotting," said Connie. "Even with a brace. That's why the town decided not to buy one."

"Well, I'm sorry," I said. "But I think the town should buy one. I bet you anything that's why the ghost spoke to me."

"Why?" asked Daisy.

"Because the tree is rotting. She must know the tree is rotting. I mean, she *lives* in that tree. I'm sure that's why she spoke to me. She wants us to help her."

"*Us?*" said Daisy.

"But how can we help?" asked Connie as she began to stack newspapers onto her cart.

"I don't know," I said.

For the next half hour or so, we walked around the neighborhood while Connie, pulling her shopping cart piled high with newspapers, went from house to house, delivering papers. All we talked about was the balm of Gilead tree and the ghost.

At one point, Connie glanced at her watch. "Good—it's not even ten o'clock. Mrs. Campbell better not complain today that her newspaper is late."

"What is it with this Mrs. Campbell?" I asked.

"She's a witch—that's what!" said Connie. "You know

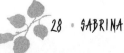

what she did last time? She called the newspaper office and complained that I delivered her paper late."

"Did you?" asked Megan.

"No!" replied Connie emphatically.

"Well, then, don't worry about it," said Megan.

Connie sighed. "You've never met Mrs. Campbell. She's so grouchy! She's the grouchiest person I've ever . . ."

Connie's voice trailed off. She stopped. "Oh, no!" she groaned. "There she is!"

We had come to a large yellow Victorian house. It had an open, wraparound front porch with white wicker furniture. An elderly woman was sitting in one of the wicker chairs, clutching a wooden cane between her legs. She was all dressed up: straw hat, sunglasses, a peach-colored summer dress.

"She doesn't look evil," said Daisy. "She looks like a sweet old lady."

"She's not sweet!" Connie said.

"Oh, for goodness' sake, Connie!" said Megan. "She's just an old lady! Here, give me a dumb newspaper. I'll go give it to her."

Connie handed her a newspaper from the cart, which had only a couple of papers left. "I'd better go with you," she said.

"Well, then, let's go," said Megan.

7 Megan

CONNIE followed me across the front lawn.

"We really shouldn't walk on her lawn," she said.

"It's just grass, Connie!"

I marched up the porch steps and walked over to where Mrs. Campbell sat in her wicker chair.

"Here's your newspaper," I announced.

Mrs. Campbell didn't say anything, so I set the newspaper down on the small wicker table beside her chair. Connie and I turned to go.

"No apology?" said Mrs. Campbell. "You're just going to leave without saying you're sorry?"

I turned and stared at her. "What are you talking about?"

"My newspaper was delivered late yesterday. I would have thought I'd hear an apology."

"First of all, I didn't deliver it," I said. "Second of all, it wasn't late."

"Nobody has any manners today," said Mrs. Campbell, shaking her head.

"I'm sorry, Mrs. Campbell," murmured Connie.

I turned and stared at Connie. "What are *you* sorry

about?" I asked. "You said you didn't deliver her newspaper late."

"Good heavens, look at that shirt!" said Mrs. Campbell disapprovingly, pointing her cane at me.

I looked down. I was wearing my pink belly shirt. "What about it?" I asked.

"It's a little skimpy, isn't it? I can see your stomach as plain as day. When I was your age, a girl would never wear such a thing."

"Well, times have changed."

"Yes, they certainly have—for the worse!"

I grabbed Connie's hand and whispered, "C'mon, Connie, let's get out of here!"

"I've got to go now, Mrs. Campbell," Connie said as I led her away.

"Of course you do," said Mrs. Campbell. "What's become of our civilization? Everybody is always so busy. It's just rush, rush, rush!"

"Boy, what a witch!" I said when we got back to Sabrina and Daisy. They were standing on the sidewalk, waiting beside Connie's newspaper cart.

"I told you, Megan!" said Connie as we continued on our way.

"If this was Salem, Massachusetts, back in the seventeenth century, she'd be burned at the stake," I said.

"I'd light the fire!" declared Connie.

We all laughed. But Connie was just talking big. She'd never light the match. She'd be too chicken.

8 Connie

OUR town library is in an old brick building covered with green ivy. On the main floor is a row of computers that you can use to find a book. You just type in a subject, a book title, or an author. The moment Sabrina, Megan, Daisy, and I walked in, Daisy ran over and grabbed a computer.

"What subject should we try?" she asked.

"Try 'ghosts,'" suggested Sabrina.

Daisy typed in "ghosts." I knew, even before she hit the return button, that we needed to narrow our search more. I was right. "Ghosts" brought up 238 entries. Daisy began to go through them, one by one, clicking.

I left Sabrina, Megan, and Daisy and walked over to the reference desk. Mrs. Rosalas, one of the librarians, was at the reference desk.

"Well, hello, Connie," she said, smiling. She knows me because I come to the library a lot with my mom.

"Hi, Mrs. Rosalas," I said. "Does the library have any books about the balm of Gilead tree that's on the village green?"

"As a matter of fact, we do," said Mrs. Rosalas. She got up and went over to the books that lined the shelves behind the reference desk. She pulled out a large book. It looked more like a family photo album than a book. A faded color photograph of the balm of Gilead tree was pasted on the front cover. The photograph was taken in autumn—the tree was ablaze with gold and yellow leaves. The book was titled *Old Balmy.*

"A local historian put this together," said Mrs. Rosalas, handing me the book. "You can't take it out of the library, dear, but you're welcome to read it at one of the tables."

"This is great!" I said. "Thanks."

I hurried back over to Sabrina, Megan, and Daisy. "Look what I found!" I said.

The other girls turned and looked at the book, then at me. They looked so amazed. "Where'd you find *that?*" asked Sabrina.

"At the reference desk."

"I would've found it on the computer sooner or later," said Daisy as we sat down at a large table by the windows to examine the book. It was divided into sections. The first section featured typewritten information about the tree. The balm of Gilead, or *Populus gileadensis,* is a variety of the balsam poplar, with twigs and triangular-shaped leaves that are somewhat hairy and about three to eight inches in size. The height of Old Balmy was roughly fifty to seventy feet, and a balm of Gilead had an average life expectancy of about seventy-five years.

But this was no average tree. This tree had lived long passed its life expectancy. Two presidents had visited the tree. One was George Washington; he slept under it. The other was Franklin Roosevelt. Back in 1932, he delivered a speech at the gazebo. In his speech, he said the tree was as old and as glorious as this great nation of ours.

The balm of Gilead was unique in another way as well. It had almost the same shape as an Eastern cottonwood, which, like the balm of Gilead, is in the Willow Family (Salicaceae). It had a massive trunk and low, thick, drooping branches that made it very inviting for children to want to climb.

The next section was made up of old black-and-white photographs. The photographs were of people posing in front of the tree.

The section after that was titled "Mrs. Rogers's Second Grade Class—1963." This section consisted of autumn leaves that had fallen from the balm of Gilead. The leaves were pressed in wax paper.

A poetry section came next. The introduction at the beginning said that the poems had been written by students in Mrs. Basil's 1972 third-grade class.

I flipped to the next section.

"Hey, what was that?" asked Sabrina.

I flipped back a few pages. Stuck in the fold of the book was an old newspaper clipping. It was all yellowed and crumbly-looking. I delicately picked it up. Some of the edges broke off when I unfolded it. The article was from *The New Elder Times*—the same newspaper I delivered. The article was dated September 25, 1932.

"Oh, my gosh!" cried Daisy. "Check out the headline!"

11-Year-Old Girl Dies in Fall from Tree

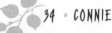

In a library whisper, I read aloud:

Sept. 25—An 11-year-old New Elder girl died late yesterday morning after she fell more than thirty feet from
the old balm of Gilead tree on the village green.

Eliza Baker, the daughter of Thomas and Mabel Baker
of 23 Edgemont Avenue, was pronounced dead at the
scene by Dr. Edmund Tanner, who was attending a cam-
paign rally at the village green for the presidential candidate Franklin Roosevelt. An autopsy determined that
Miss Baker died of a severe concussion to the brain.

Eliza Baker had climbed the tree with another local
girl, Ginny Doyle, the daughter of James and Ruth Doyle
of 25 Edgemont Avenue. According to Sheriff Stanley
Hunter, the two friends ascended the tree in the hope
of getting a better view of Franklin Roosevelt, who was
about to speak at the gazebo on the village green.

Eliza Baker, an only child, was a fifth-grade student
at the New Elder Elementary School. A funeral service
will be held on Friday morning at the Congregational
church on Elm Street.

The article included a small black-and-white photograph,
a headshot of a smiling girl. She looked a little like Shirley
Temple. She had a big bow in her hair and corkscrew curls.

"That's our ghost!" said Daisy.

And the ghost had a name—Eliza Baker.

"She was only eleven when she died," said Megan.

"Our age," I said.

9 Daisy

BEFORE we left the library, Sabrina took out some of the books that her mother wanted her to read over the summer. As we rode our bikes back to Sabrina's house to get lunch, all we talked about was Eliza Baker.

"I can't believe she was our age!" I said.

"I can't believe she went to our school!" said Sabrina, who was riding her bike one-handed. Her other hand was holding the bag of library books.

"That photograph really creeped me out!" said Connie. "I can't get Eliza Baker's face out of my mind!"

"I still can't believe she was our age!" I said.

"Daisy, that's the fifth time you've said that!" Megan cried.

"Well, I can't help it if I can't believe it!" I said.

When we got to Sabrina's house, we made ourselves some tuna-fish sandwiches for lunch. Well, not all of us. Megan didn't eat tuna fish—she was a vegetarian. She had a Rockin' Raspberry yogurt instead.

"So what do you think we should do?" Sabrina asked as we sat around her kitchen table, eating.

"What do you mean?" asked Connie.

"About Eliza," replied Sabrina. "She asked us to help her. The balm of Gilead tree is about to be cut down. That tree is her home. It's where she died. Obviously, she wants us to help save her home."

"Sabrina, the tree is rotting," I said. "There's not much we can do."

Sabrina thought for a moment. "What if *we* bought a brace for the balm of Gilead tree?" she asked.

I thought Sabrina was kidding. "Oh, yeah, sure," I said. "Let's go buy one!"

"I'm serious, Daisy! What if we bought a brace for the tree?"

"Earth to Sabrina," said Megan. "A brace costs six thousand dollars."

"Well . . . we could raise it," suggested Sabrina.

"Raise it?" Connie asked doubtfully.

"Sabrina, we're talking thousands of dollars!" said Megan. "There's no way four fifth-grade girls can raise that kind of money!"

"How do we know unless we try?" Sabrina asked.

"I agree with Sabrina," I said. "I think we should try."

"Come on, Daisy, be real—there's no way we can raise that kind of money," Megan argued. "We'll just be wasting our time."

"But Eliza is depending on us," Sabrina insisted. "She asked us to help her!"

"So you say," said Megan.

"What? You don't believe I heard a girl's voice?"

"All I know is I was at the tree last night, too, and I didn't hear a thing," Megan said.

"But Connie says it's not unusual for only one person to hear a ghost."

"Maybe Connie is wrong," I said.

"I'm not wrong, Daisy."

"Look, Meggy," said Sabrina. "Maybe you're right. Maybe we can't raise the whole thing. But we can at least try!"

"Sabrina's right!" I cried. I leaped up from the table and grabbed a pad and a pencil from the kitchen counter. "Here," I said, handing them to Sabrina. "Let's write down ideas."

"Okay, what's one thing we can do?" Sabrina asked.

"Hello! We're on summer vacation, remember?" said Megan. "We're supposed to be relaxing and having fun."

Just then, as Megan was saying this, Sabrina's mother walked into the kitchen with a ceramic coffee cup in her hand. She had on denim shorts and a T-shirt that said FREE TIBET NOW! across the front. Mrs. Ingalls, who worked at home, was very big into causes.

"You girls are going to clean up your mess when you're through, right?" Mrs. Ingalls said. She poured herself some coffee from the coffeemaker on the counter. Then she said, "What are you girls up to?"

"We're figuring out how to raise money to buy a brace for the balm of Gilead tree!" I said.

The moment I said it, I felt someone step on my foot. Sabrina. She shook her head at me not to say anything.

"Oops! Sorry!" I whispered. I put my hand over my mouth so I wouldn't blurt out any more secrets. But the damage had already been done.

"That's great you're raising money, Sabrina," said Mrs. Ingalls. "I hope you really do it."

"I'll do it," said Sabrina.

"Uh-huh."

"I will!"

"You don't even do the chores I give you so you can have allowance money. How do you expect to raise money to buy a brace?"

"I guess you'll just have to find out," said Sabrina.

"How do you know the town even wants you to raise money to buy a brace?" asked Mrs. Ingalls.

"Good question!" replied Megan. "We don't!"

"I'm sure people will be more than happy when they find out we want to buy a brace for the balm of Gilead tree," said Sabrina.

"What kind of fund-raising event are you thinking of?" asked Mrs. Ingalls.

"We don't know yet," said Sabrina. "Now good-bye!"

"You could always hold a bikeathon," Mrs. Ingalls suggested.

"Everybody and his brother does a bikeathon," Sabrina said. "I was hoping we could think of something a little more imaginative."

"Imaginative, you say?" said Mrs. Ingalls. "Hmm . . ." She leaned against the kitchen counter and took a sip from her coffee cup. "You know, back in the mid-1980s, there was a big nationwide effort to help the homeless. Oh, what was it called?"

"Well, when you think of it, come back and tell us," said Sabrina.

"Hands Across America!" cried Mrs. Ingalls. "People from all across the country came together for one day and raised money for the homeless by holding hands and forming one long continuous chain of people. The chain was suppose to stretch from coast to coast—"

"You mean from New York to California?" I asked.

"It was supposed to," said Mrs. Ingalls. "I'm not sure that actually happened, but I do think quite a bit of money was raised. Anyone who wanted to be in the chain was asked to donate money. Your father and I took part in it."

"Cool!" I said. "I think we should do it. Write it down, Sabrina."

But Sabrina didn't. "I think we should talk it over," she said.

"Here, I'll write it down." I grabbed the pad and pencil, but the pencil flew out of my hand and fell onto the floor.

"I'll get it," said Megan, bending down. She disappeared under the table for a moment, then reappeared with the pencil. "I hate to tell you this, Daisy, but your socks don't match."

"I know," I said.

"You *know?*" said Megan. She looked horrified. Of the four of us, Megan was the most into fashion. She had more clothes than the three of us put together. She was also the only one of us who had pierced ears, wore rings, and used finger- and toenail polish on a regular basis (and used really wild colors, too). She wasn't a girly-girl, though.

"I couldn't find socks that matched," I explained. "I guess they got lost in the dryer."

"Don't you have any other socks you could've worn?" asked Megan.

"Duh! Of course I do," I replied. "But I like these socks. So rather than never wear the socks again, I decided to wear them together. Don't you hate it when you lose a sock in the dryer? You never lose both socks. Just one."

"I must have a dozen socks in my dresser that don't match," said Connie.

"Everyone does," said Sabrina.

Then, all of a sudden, the most brilliant idea popped into my head.

"I've got it!" I cried out.

"Got what?" asked Megan.

"The big idea!" I said. "I know how we can raise money! We'll hold a sockathon!"

10 Sabrina

I DON'T know what it is about my mother, but she can't keep herself from always butting in with suggestions about my life. But if she hadn't butted in, Daisy would never have come up with the idea of the sockathon.

Megan, frowning, said, "A *what?*"

"A sockathon!"

"What's a sockathon?" asked Connie.

"It's like that Hands Across America thing, but with socks."

"How does it work?" I asked.

"People will donate socks that they no longer wear because the other sock got lost in the dryer."

"We're going to ask people to donate their old, dirty socks?" said Megan, horrified.

"No! Just clean socks," said Daisy. "We'll insist they have to be clean. When people donate socks, they'll also donate money. We'll tie all the socks people donate to us and make a chain and string it across town. You know, like Hands Across America."

"Hey, and we can call it Socks Across Town!" said Megan.

"No, I think Sockathon is better," said Daisy. She didn't realize Megan was just being sarcastic. "So what do you think, guys?" she asked, her eyes glistening with excitement.

"I think you've lost your mind," said Megan.

My mother had been listening without saying anything. Until now. "It's a wonderfully imaginative idea," she said. "But I think it may be a little—"

Megan cut in: "Weird?"

"Actually," said my mother, "I was going to say I think it may be a little difficult to get people to donate enough socks."

Daisy looked hurt. I could tell she was upset. It really bothered Daisy when people didn't take her ideas seriously. Kids in school were always making fun of her because they thought she was weird.

"Oh, well," she sighed, pushing the pad and pencil across the table toward me. "It was just a thought."

"Why *don't* you girls do something like Hands Across America," said my mother. "What do you think?"

I'll tell you what I thought. I was sick and tired of my mother butting in. I was also mad at her for hurting Daisy's feelings. "Actually," I said, "I like Daisy's idea."

Megan, Connie, and Daisy all stared at me. They looked stunned. Daisy looked the most stunned of all.

"You do?" she said.

I nodded and said, "I do. I like it a lot. It's different."

"It's different, all right," agreed Megan.

"You're not serious, are you?" Connie asked me.

"Yeah, I am," I replied. "I think it's a great idea. People will want to donate money to have their socks in our sock chain. You know why I like this idea so much?"

"Why?" asked Daisy.

"Because once the balm of Gilead is cut down, it's lost forever," I said. "Like a sock that's been lost in the dryer."

Daisy gazed at me as though I had said something terribly brilliant. "That is *so* true," she said.

"I don't know about this, Sabrina," said Connie.

"Yeah, handling a bunch of smelly old socks isn't exactly my idea of a fun summer vacation," said Megan.

"They won't be smelly," I said. "Like Daisy said, we'll insist that all donated socks have to be clean."

"I say we vote on it," said Daisy.

"Vote on what?" said Megan.

"All those in favor of holding a sockathon, raise your hand," commanded Daisy.

Daisy's hand shot up like a missile. I raised my hand. Megan sat on both her hands. That left just Connie.

"Come on, Connie, raise your hand!" said Daisy.

Connie was on the spot. She looked extremely uncomfortable. She had to choose one friend over another. Connie hated making decisions like this. Biting her bottom lip, Connie glanced at Megan. Then she glanced at Daisy and me, then back at Megan. I could guess what was going through Connie's mind: that there were two of us and only one of Megan. Connie slowly, hesitantly, lifted her hand. She turned to Megan and said, "Sorry."

"Yesss!" exclaimed Daisy, throwing her fist up in the air. "Three to one! We win!"

I turned to my mother and said, "I guess we're having a sockathon!"

I knew I was being flip, but you know what? I didn't care. I really didn't.

"I guess you are," replied my mother. "Well, best of luck, girls." She picked up her coffee mug and walked out of the kitchen.

"I've got to tell you, guys," said Megan, "this is the worst idea I have ever heard of. I mean, this idea is pure looney tunes."

"Whose house should we have people send their socks to?" asked Daisy.

"Not mine," replied Megan.

"I don't think my dad would be too crazy if it was my house, either," said Daisy.

"Hey, what about Denver?" asked Connie, looking at me. "He might be able to help us."

"Denver? *Who's* Denver?" asked Daisy.

"Our minister," I said.

Like mine, Connie's family belonged to the Congregational church in town. We never saw each other in church, though. That's because my family attended the 8:30 service, while Connie's family went to the 10:30.

"He's a really nice guy," said Connie. "I'm sure he'd be able to help us."

My mother came back into the kitchen. She had a bunch of white and colored socks in her hand.

"Let me be the first to make a donation," she said. She dumped the socks on the kitchen table, right in front of me. Then she dropped two dollars on top of the socks.

Megan placed her hands over her face as if she had a terrific headache. "Oh, no!" she moaned. "It's really happening!"

11 Megan

AFTER we left Sabrina's house, Daisy was practically foaming at the mouth, she was so excited about her sockathon idea. We rode our bikes into town and parked them in front of the Congregational church. The big, old, white, steepled building stood near the village green, just across the street from the balm of Gilead tree.

Sabrina and Connie led the way through the church to where the offices were located. An elderly woman with white hair and glasses was at a desk, typing at a computer.

"Hello," she said, smiling sweetly, when we walked in. "Can I help you?"

"We're looking for Denver," said Sabrina.

"He stepped out for a minute. Is there something I can help you with?"

"We really need to speak with Denver," said Sabrina.

"Well, he'll be back soon," the woman said. "If you like, you can wait in his office."

She showed us into a large office that looked out on the church cemetery.

What a lovely view, I thought.

I sat down between Sabrina and Connie on a kind of ratty-looking couch that was beside a large bookcase crammed with books. All the books had religious-sounding titles. Daisy plopped down in an armchair facing the minister's desk. An autographed baseball sat on a small wooden cradle on the desk. Daisy picked up the baseball and squinted at the name scribbled in blue ink on its white surface.

"Anyone ever hear of a Tug McGraw?" she asked.

None of us had.

"Listen to what he wrote," said Daisy. "'Ya gotta believe.'"

"What does that mean?" I asked.

None of us knew.

12 Connie

I DIDN'T like Daisy touching Denver's stuff. It made me nervous. I was worried Denver might walk in and—

"Aha! Caught you playing with my prized possession!" It was Denver. He was a large, balding man with a big, booming voice. Usually when I see Denver, it's on a Sunday morning when he's dressed in a white robe. But that day he didn't look at all like a minister. He had on khaki pants, a green polo shirt, and blue sneakers.

"I was just looking at it," said Daisy as she quickly put the ball back.

"Know what I do to people who I catch fiddling with my Tug McGraw autographed baseball?" Denver asked.

Daisy looked very tense. "What?"

"I make them listen to how I got it."

We all laughed. I sat back and relaxed. That's what I loved about Denver. He was always kidding. Sabrina introduced Denver to Daisy and Megan, and then Denver sat down at his desk and said, "I caught this baseball at Shea Stadium back in August, 1973, when the Mets were playing the Pittsburgh Pirates. The Mets' ace relief pitcher Tug

McGraw pitched this ball in the top half of the ninth inning, with two men on and one out. The great Willie Stargell was up. He hit it foul—one of those high rocket blasts into the upper stands. Yours truly, sitting in section two, caught the ball. After the game, I waited for Tug McGraw out in the parking lot and asked him to sign it."

"Why did he sign it 'Ya gotta believe'?" Daisy asked.

Denver stared at Daisy. He had the most incredulous expression on his face. "You mean to tell me you're not familiar with Tug McGraw's famous saying?"

Daisy shook her head.

"Connie, tell your friend why Tug McGraw said 'Ya gotta believe,'" said Denver.

"I don't know why," I replied.

Denver gave me a shocked look. "Sabrina, will you kindly tell your friends why Tug McGraw said 'Ya gotta believe'?"

"I don't know either, Denver."

Denver turned to Megan.

Megan shook her head before he even spoke.

"I can't believe none of you guys have ever heard Tug McGraw's famous saying," said Denver.

"So why did he say it?" asked Megan.

"Well," said Denver. "The Mets hadn't been playing very well that year. They were so far out of first place in July, nobody thought they had much of a chance to win their division, let alone be in the World Series. But the Mets believed in themselves. They believed they could win. And do you know what?"

"What?" asked Megan.

"They made it into the World Series."

"Did they win?" I asked.

"Well, no—but they got in." Denver, smiling, folded his hands on his desk and said, "So, tell me, young ladies, how can I help you?"

"Well," said Sabrina. "You've heard how the town wants to cut down the old balm of Gilead tree, haven't you?"

"Oh, yes," said Denver. "Such a shame."

"We want to save the tree!" Daisy blurted out.

Sabrina nodded. "We want to buy a brace for the tree."

"That's very generous of you," said Denver.

"Wait'll you hear *how* we intend to raise the money," said Daisy.

Denver, leaning forward, asked, "How do you intend to raise it?"

"We're going to hold a sockathon!" said Daisy.

"A *sockathon?*" Denver said. "I've heard of bikeathons and walkathons, but I've never heard of a sockathon. What is it?"

Daisy told him. She couldn't resist telling him it was *her* idea. Denver roared with laughter. "I love it!" he cried.

"You do?" Megan looked shocked.

"It's the most original fund-raiser I have ever heard of," he said. "Boy, this sure beats our potluck dinners."

"Thank you." Daisy beamed.

"Anyway," said Sabrina, "we need a place where people can bring their socks."

"How about here?" volunteered Denver.

"We don't want to put you to any trouble," Megan insisted.

"It's no trouble," said Denver. "In fact, it makes perfect sense. You'll be right across from the balm of Gilead tree. But I do have a question for you."

"What's that?" asked Sabrina.

"Have you gotten the town's permission to hold a sock-athon?"

"Why, no, we haven't," said Megan. "Do you think that'll be a problem?"

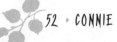

13 Daisy

OH-OH, I thought when Denver asked us if we had the town's approval to hold our fund-raiser. *So much for our sockathon!*

"Who should we talk to?" asked Sabrina.

"The mayor, Nancy Sargent," he replied.

"You want *us* to talk to the mayor?" I cried, startled.

"Well, considering you want to string socks all over town, I think it might be a good idea," said Denver. "She happens to be a parishioner of this church. If you like, I can give her a call. See if I can set up a meeting so you can tell her your idea."

"We don't want you to go to any trouble," said Megan.

"It's no trouble."

"Well, if you don't mind," said Sabrina, "that would be great."

Denver picked up the phone and called the mayor's office. But Mrs. Sargent was in a meeting. After he got off the phone, Denver told us that Mrs. Sargent was going to call back in about ten minutes. Denver said we could wait in his office, but Sabrina said no, we'd wait outside. I think she was worried we were taking up too much of Denver's time.

We went out the side door of the church to wait. The shady lawn had recently been mowed—the air smelled of freshly cut grass. At the edge of the lawn was a flower garden in bloom. Just beyond the garden was a white picket fence. And just beyond that . . . the church cemetery.

The graves looked really old. I was curious to see how old they were, so I opened the gate and stepped into the cemetery.

"What are you doing, Daisy?" asked Connie. She sounded alarmed. Like I was doing something that was going to get us into big trouble.

"I just want to look at the graves," I said. I stopped in front of a crooked, reddish-brown headstone. It had a spooky face chiseled near the top.

"Whoa!" I said. "This grave is from 1832!"

Sabrina and Megan followed me into the cemetery. But not Connie. I guess she was too scared.

"Hey, this one is even older!" said Sabrina, stopping at another crooked headstone. "It's from 1810!"

Megan walked over to a small headstone that was at the edge of the cemetery, near the street. It had a clump of purple lilacs on the grave. The headstone looked much newer than the other gravestones in this part of the cemetery. The front of the slab had a smooth, glassy surface.

"This grave isn't very old," she said. "The guy died in 1992. Listen to what it says on his gravestone: 'Gatherer of Friends.' What do you suppose *that* means?"

I shrugged and said, "Got me."

"Hey, guys, I just thought of something!" said Connie. She had entered the cemetery. She must have gotten over her nervousness. "That old newspaper article said that Eliza Baker's funeral was at the Congregational church. Maybe Eliza Baker is buried right here in this cemetery."

We stopped and glanced at one another, then at the headstones all about us. It was as if someone had shouted "Go!" All at once, we split up. Each of us dashed from headstone to headstone, searching for Eliza Baker's grave. It was a race to see who could find the gravestone first. If Eliza Baker was buried in this cemetery, I wanted to be the first one to find the grave. The first one to say . . .

"I found it!" shouted Connie.

She was standing over on a ridge, under a shady tree, in front of a small headstone.

We all ran over to where Connie stood. She pointed to the headstone. It said:

Eliza Katherine Baker
1921–1932

"Whoa!" I cried. "How did you find it so fast?"

"I don't know," said Connie. "I just had a strange feeling that this was where it was going to be."

Sabrina glanced around at all the graves around us. She looked a little nervous. "It's kind of spooky being here," she said.

Connie began to act weird. She bent down and touched

the grass that was growing on Eliza Baker's grave. It was as if she was in a trance or something.

Just then, across the cemetery, I spotted Denver outside the church.

"Here we are, Denver!" I shouted, waving.

"So this is where you all disappeared to," Denver said as we came walking out of the cemetery.

"Did you speak with Mrs. Sargent?" asked Sabrina.

"I did," said Denver.

"And?" I asked.

"She'd be more than happy to meet with you. In fact, she said she could meet with you right now for a few minutes."

"Now?" said Sabrina.

"Awesome!" I cried.

"Guys, she's never going to agree to a sockathon," Megan warned.

"Hey, ya gotta believe!" I said.

I glanced at Denver. He winked.

14 Sabrina

THE mayor's office was in Town Hall—an old brick building that stood at the south end of the village green. It was only a five-minute walk from the Congregational church. While we walked, Daisy, Connie, and Megan couldn't stop talking about Eliza Baker's grave. Particularly Daisy. Not me, though. I hardly said a word. I was thinking about meeting with the mayor.

"Okay, guys, we need to focus on what we're going to say to the mayor," I said as we entered the Town Hall building.

While we waited in the lobby for the elevator to take us upstairs, we decided that only one of us should do the talking. Connie, Daisy, and Megan said it should be me.

"Why me?" I asked.

"It was your idea to try and save the tree," said Megan.

As we headed up in the elevator, I started to get nervous. "Remember, not a word about Eliza Baker," I whispered. I said it to everyone, but it was really Daisy who worried me. I knew Connie and Megan wouldn't say anything.

The mayor's assistant was a young, skinny guy with curly hair and a pimply face. He led us into a room with a long, shiny, wooden conference table. As soon as he left us, Daisy opened her eyes wide and said, "He was cute!"

Megan frowned. "You call *him* cute?"

"You didn't think he was cute?" asked Daisy.

Megan frowned even more.

A tall, slim, middle-aged woman in a business suit strode into the room. "Hello, I'm Nancy Sargent," she said, and shook each of our hands.

We each introduced ourselves. Then Mrs. Sargent got right down to business. I guess she wasn't one for small talk. In a way, she kind of reminded me of my mother.

"So tell me about this fund-raising event you'd like to hold," she said, taking a seat beside Daisy. "I think Denver said you were calling it a sockathon?"

"Yes," I said. I explained to her how it was going to work. I expected her to laugh. But she didn't. She didn't even smile. She took it very seriously. She immediately began questioning how the sockathon would work.

"What will you do when you come to a driveway or the entrance to a parking lot?" she asked.

I didn't know. We hadn't thought about that. What *would* we do when we came to a driveway or a parking-lot entrance? Would we have the sock chain cross over it? But if we did that, the sock chain would get run over by cars and trucks.

"Um, gee that's a good question," I said, but I thought, *Oh, great! Now I've blown it! Mrs. Sargent is going to think we haven't thought out our idea.*

To my surprise, though, Mrs. Sargent came up with a solution!

"Well, I suppose every time you came to a driveway or a parking-lot entrance, you could end the sock chain. Then you could have it resume on the other side. On the last day of the sockathon, there could be a big event when all the ends of the sock chain are tied together. We could make it into a big street fair. People could join together to connect all the pieces to make it one long continuous sock chain."

"Cool!" exclaimed Daisy.

"I have another question for you," said Mrs. Sargent. "It's summer and you're off from school. I'm sure you have a lot going on. Do you girls think you will stick with it?"

Boy, she sounded just like my mother!

"We sure will!" I said.

"How about vacations?" she said. "Aren't you girls going to camp or anywhere with your families this summer?"

"My family went to Florida during spring break," I said. "That was our vacation for the year."

"My family is going to Cape Cod, but only for about a week," said Daisy.

"We're hoping to go to China," said Connie. "But that's not till the end of the year."

"My mom and I are just hanging out this summer," said Megan. "She's kind of worried about her job."

Mrs. Sargent folded her hands on the table. "I think it's very noble of you girls to want to buy a brace for the tree," she said. "You're aware, of course, that a brace isn't going to heal the tree. The tree is going to keep right on rotting."

"Yes, we know that," I said. "But the balm of Gilead tree

is over two hundred and seventy-five years old! George Washington slept under it! You can't just cut it down!"

"Well, you're not the only ones who feel this way," said Mrs. Sargent. "Since we announced our plan to cut down the tree, this office has been deluged with phone calls and e-mails from people who feel the same way you girls do. They think we should do everything possible to save the tree."

"So why don't you?" I asked.

"Well, for starters, we don't have the money," said Mrs. Sargent. "This town is operating on a deficit. We have no money in our budget to buy a brace, which is why your sockathon idea intrigues me so much."

"It does?" said Megan.

"It's such a wonderfully creative idea," said Mrs. Sargent. "It's bound to give our town some positive publicity."

"Lots of positive publicity!" said Daisy.

"I also like the fact that you four girls wish to volunteer your service to help out our community," said Mrs. Sargent. "I'm a strong believer in volunteerism. It's something I feel should be encouraged. You're never too young to get involved, I believe."

"So does that mean we can do it?" I asked.

Mrs. Sargent was quiet for a moment. Then she said, "Yes—but we'll all have to agree on a few things. First of all, we'll have to set a time limit to your sockathon. The sockathon will have to be over before school resumes. So let's say it'll end on Labor Day weekend. Also, once the sockathon is over, you girls will be responsible for cleaning up the socks."

"Don't worry! We will!" said Daisy.

"I'm sure Goodwill or the Salvation Army would be happy to get the socks," said Mrs. Sargent. "And, finally, if people say they don't want the sock chain running in front of their house or store, you'll have to honor their wishes. We don't want anyone getting upset."

"We'll do whatever anybody asks," I promised.

Mrs. Sargent glanced at her watch, then rose from her chair. "I'm afraid I have another meeting to rush off to," she said. She shook each of our hands again. "Well, best of luck, girls."

"I'm going to make sure my parents vote for you in November!" declared Daisy.

For the first time, Mrs. Sargent smiled. "That's very nice of you, dear. Except I'm not up for reelection this year."

I didn't say a word to my mother about our meeting with Denver or with Mrs. Sargent. I wanted it to be a surprise. I knew she thought that I wouldn't stick with the sockathon. I knew she thought it'd be like me doing my chores to earn allowance money—that I'd grow bored with it after a while and stop. I was always disappointing my mother. (Not like my older sister, Jill, who's in college. She not only gets excellent grades, but that summer she had a summer job teaching kids how to read on an Indian reservation in Arizona.) My mother thought I didn't try hard enough. That I didn't give things my very best effort. She told me so herself. Well, I wanted to prove to my mother just how wrong she was.

When Sunday came around, my family did what we usually do on Sunday mornings. We went to church. As usual, we were about ten minutes late. When we pulled into the church parking lot, Daddy, as usual, parked in front of the Sunday-school classrooms. We walked into church during the Greeting part of the service, when everyone gets up and walks around and greets one another, saying things like "Good morning" and "Peace be with you" as they hug and shake hands. I just stood in my pew and thought about Eliza Baker.

This is where her funeral took place.

After the Greeting, Denver, as usual, stood at the front of the church and asked, "Are there any concerns or announcements?"

And that's when things stopped happening as usual.

A plump woman with dyed blond hair stood up and announced that her mother was having a hip replacement and that she needed our prayers.

"Any other concerns or announcements?" asked Denver, glancing around. His gaze fell upon me. "Sabrina, you have an announcement to make, don't you?"

My mother and father turned and stared at me. They looked shocked. I almost burst out laughing at their startled faces. Particularly my mother's. I rose to my feet. Denver had told me he was going to ask me to get up and speak in church. In my most solemn voice, I said, "Yes, I do."

I told the congregation about how Daisy, Connie, Megan, and I were raising money to buy a brace for the balm of Gilead tree. I heard some chuckles when I explained how we intended to raise the money. I didn't say anything about Eliza Baker, of course.

Then Denver said, "The girls have put a big cardboard box outside my office in case anyone wishes to donate socks. They've also put out a shoebox, in case you wish to donate money to buy a brace for the balm of Gilead—which I certainly hope you'll do."

I sat down. My mother, looking straight ahead, leaned sideways toward me and whispered, "I didn't know you spoke to Denver."

"There are a lot of things you don't know about me," I replied.

"When did you speak with Denver?"

"Oh, just before we spoke to the mayor."

My mother turned her head and stared at me. "You spoke to the mayor?"

I didn't say anything. I just smiled and reached for the red hymnal that was in the rack on the back of the pew in front of me. Denver had asked us to open to Hymn 64.

We all stood up and sang, "For the beauty of the earth, for the glory of the skies . . ."

I had shocked my mother. She had thought she knew me inside and out, but I had shown her that she really didn't.

15 Megan

WHEN I found out that Sabrina had made an announcement in church about the sockathon, I thought, *Now we'll be flooded with millions of socks!*

But it didn't happen.

In fact, only a few people donated socks during the next couple of days. There were maybe sixty socks, if that, in the big cardboard box we had placed outside Denver's office.

At this rate, the sockathon will be over in a week, I thought happily.

Don't get me wrong. It wasn't that I didn't want to help raise money to buy a brace for the balm of Gilead tree. I just didn't want to do it during my summer vacation when I was supposed to be having fun. And to be honest, I also wasn't crazy about doing the sockathon. I mean, talk about wacky ideas! I could just hear the kids—especially the boys—teasing us when we got back to school in September.

That night being a Tuesday, Mom and I went to the nursing home to visit Great-aunt Carrie.

I hated visiting Great-aunt Carrie. Just hated it. I hated the nursing home. I hated the smell inside the building—it smelled like old people. I hated seeing all the old people who lived there. They were so wrinkled and frail. But most of all, I hated seeing Great-aunt Carrie. She was just skin and bones. She never said a word to us. Not even a "hello." She just lay in her bed and stared at us.

On the way home from the nursing home, Mom and I stopped and ate at a diner. We sat down in a booth by the cash register. A skinny, college-age girl with punky purply blond hair waited on us. She had a small silver ring in her left eyebrow. I couldn't stop staring at it.

Mom noticed me staring. After our waitress took our order, Mom leaned forward and said, "Don't even think about piercing your eyebrow—or any other part of your body."

"But *Mom!*" I protested. I was just kidding around.

"But *no!*"

"What about a tattoo?"

"No!"

"I bet *you* would've gotten one when you were a teen-ager," I said. Mom used to be very rebellious when she was younger. She told me so herself.

"I would have asked my mother first," she said.

"Yeah, right," I said.

Mom smiled—or sort of smiled. She looked really beat. She had had a rough day at work, I could tell.

The waitress came with the tea Mom had ordered. I watched as Mom squeezed the lemon slice into her mug.

"Since it's summer and all," I said, "what do you say we take a little break from visiting Great-aunt Carrie?"

"Why would we want to do that?" asked Mom.

"Why not?" I replied. "It's not like Great-aunt Carrie even knows who we are. I mean, she just lies there in her bed. She never even says a word to us."

"She knows we're there," said Mom.

"How do you know?" I asked. "Has she *ever* spoken?"

"Of course she's spoken, Megan."

"Recently?"

Mom didn't answer. She knew I knew the answer: no. Great-aunt Carrie hadn't spoken in ages.

"Megan," said Mom, "like it or not, it's important we visit Great-aunt Carrie each week. If we didn't, no one would. Now let's drop the subject, okay?"

"Fine," I said. "But if you ask me, I think it's a total waste of our time."

Neither one of us spoke for a while. Mom just sipped her tea. Finally the waitress came with my glass of root beer.

"So how come you had to work late?" I asked.

Mom let out a weary sigh. She had been over an hour late. "I was trying to come up with a new promotion for the radio station."

"Maybe I can help," I said. I stuck my straw into my root beer and took a sip. "What kind of a new promotion are you looking for?"

Mom groaned. "I wish I knew. Fred hasn't liked a single one of my ideas."

Fred was her boss. He had come to the radio station about five months ago. According to Mom, he had been hired to shake things up at the station, with the goal of improving ratings. From what I could tell, the only goal he had achieved so far was to make Mom's life miserable.

"What's his problem?" I said.

"He wants a big idea," replied Mom. "An idea that's going to, as he puts it, knock the socks off our listeners."

I held up my hands, palms out. *"Please!"* I said. "Don't mention that word."

"What word?" asked Mom.

"Socks," I replied. "I don't want to be reminded of the sockathon."

"The *what?*"

"Oh, didn't I tell you?" I said. "Sabrina, Connie, Daisy, and I are having a big sockathon this summer."

"What on earth is a *sockathon?*"

"You mean *you* don't know what a sockathon is? Come on, Mom, get with the program!"

Mom smiled. "What's a sockathon?"

I told her. She was very impressed when she heard we had met with the mayor.

Mom said, "Why are you girls doing this?"

"Sabrina wants to buy a brace for the old balm of Gilead tree that's on the village green." I didn't tell Mom about Eliza Baker. I was sworn to secrecy. I had made a pinkie promise.

"You girls are raising money to save the balm of Gilead tree?" said Mom. "That's so nice of you."

I rolled my eyes.

"How much money have you raised so far?"

"I don't know. Maybe fifteen dollars."

"And how much does a brace cost?"

Mom whistled when I told her.

The waitress returned with our dinner. She was holding two oval plates, one in each hand. She set the grilled cheese down in front of me. Then she gave Mom her plate.

"So tell me more about this sockathon," said Mom as she picked her hamburger up to take a bite.

16 Connie

I KNOW this sounds really strange, but I was sure that my finding Eliza Baker's grave was some kind of sign.

Here's why: The four of us—Megan, Sabrina, Daisy, and I—were all wandering around in the cemetery that morning. Any one of us could have stumbled upon Eliza Baker's grave. But only *I* did. Not only that, but just before I walked over to the headstone, I had this funny feeling that it was her grave. I don't know why, but I did. I just knew it belonged to Eliza Baker.

Is that weird or what?

I couldn't stop thinking about Eliza Baker and how she had spoken to Sabrina. *Would Eliza ever speak again?* I wondered. If she did, would it again be to Sabrina? Or one of the rest of us? If only she would speak to me!

After Mrs. Sargent gave us permission to hold our sockathon, we put up a big poster in front of the balm of Gilead tree that announced the sockathon. During the day, we sat in the shade of the balm of Gilead tree and stapled socks that had been donated the day before.

When we ran out of socks to staple, Megan and I tied one end of the sock chain to the balm of Gilead's enormous trunk. Then Daisy and Connie took the other end of the sock chain and began to walk away from the tree, across the grass, into the blazing afternoon sunshine. They pulled the sock chain behind them like it was a garden hose. Past the gazebo. Past the statue of the Civil War soldier. They got almost to the flagpole that stood in the middle of the village green when the sock chain came to an end. Daisy made a little sign that she stuck in the ground where the sock chain ended. It said:

TO BE CONTINUED . . .

One morning while we were all sitting around under the tree, stapling socks, I discovered something else I was sure was some sort of sign meant just for me. As I was stapling, I was being careful to vary the colors of my socks, the way you would a string of Christmas tree lights. I didn't want two socks of the same color next to each other. I had stapled a red sock, a green sock, a white sock, a yellow sock. Now I needed a blue sock. I saw that Megan had a blue sock she was about to staple.

"Hey, Meg, could I have that sock?" I said.

Megan tossed it to me. Too far. The sock landed at the foot of the tree. Right near a big root. As I leaned over to pick it up, I spotted my second sign.

It was hard to see, it was so faint. It had been carved in a small oval opening in the bark, a few inches up from the ground:

Eliza and Ginny
5-11-31
Friends to the End

I stared, gasped, pointed, shrieked: "Guys, look!"

17 Daisy

CONNIE got so excited after she found Eliza and Ginny's names carved into the trunk of the old balm of Gilead tree, it was as if she had discovered a prehistoric fossil. Usually, I'm the one who gets all carried away. Not this time. This time it was Connie.

"This is so amazing!" she kept saying.

"I don't think it's so amazing," I said. "I think it's kind of sad."

Connie, frowning, said, *"Sad?* Why is it sad?"

"Think about it, Connie," I said. "That old newspaper article said Eliza Baker died in 1932." I pointed to the tree. "It says here 1931. That means Eliza had only one year left of her life. When they wrote 'Friends to the End,' things really were about to end!"

"I hadn't thought of that," said Connie.

"What do you suppose happened to Eliza's friend, Ginny?" asked Sabrina.

"She's probably long dead," said Megan.

For the next few days, I just kept thinking about that saying—"Friends to the End." It made me so sad. I kept seeing these two girls, kneeling by the tree, carving their names into the bark, not knowing how soon things would end for one of them. But that wasn't the only thing that was on my mind. There was something else that I worried was about to end.

Our sockathon.

Here's why—nobody was donating socks. Or money. After Sabrina made an announcement in her church about the sockathon, I thought that we would be swamped with socks and donations. But we weren't. I was so bummed out.

Not only that, every night I was going on the Internet and telling chat rooms about the sockathon. I thought for sure that would get people to send us socks and money. But it didn't.

The sockathon was very important to me. It was my idea, my big brainstorm. I did not want it to fizzle out. I didn't want people to say: "What did you expect? It was a ditzy idea! And no wonder: it was Daisy *Deitz* who thought of it!"

I wanted this idea to be a success—a huge, smashing success!

On the Wednesday just before the Fourth of July—a hot, sticky, hazy afternoon—we were out on the village green, stapling the few socks that people had donated, when Megan's cell phone rang. Megan was the only one of us who had a cell phone. Her mother had gotten it for her a few days after September 11. She wanted Megan to have it, she said, in case there was ever an emergency.

"Where am I?" said Megan, speaking into the slim cell phone. "I'm on the village green. Why?"

Megan listened for a moment, then said, "Okay, okay! I'll find a radio!"

"What's up?" Sabrina asked as Megan put away her cell phone.

"My mom wants us to find a radio."

"Why?" I asked.

Megan shrugged. "She didn't say. She just said to find a radio as soon as possible and tune it to WBAZ-FM."

Connie pointed to a woman in a white tennis outfit over on Elm Street. She was just getting out of a dark green SUV. "Maybe that lady will let us listen to her car radio," she said.

We dashed over. The woman was locking the front door when we came rushing up.

"Wait! Wait! Wait!" I shouted, waving my arms. "Can we listen to your radio?"

The woman whirled about. She looked very startled. "My radio?" she asked.

"Your car radio," said Sabrina.

"Can we listen to it?" asked Connie.

"Please!" I said. Dropping to my knees, I clasped my hands like I was begging.

"See, my mom works at a radio station," explained Megan. "She just called and said to listen to the station."

The woman smiled, sort of, and said, "Sure, I guess so."

The woman got back into her car and turned on the radio. It was set to a classical music station. A piano concerto was playing. Megan told her where WBAZ-FM was.

A commercial for a breath mint was being broadcast. It

ended, and then a DJ came on the air, talking about the salami-and-onion sandwich he had just had for lunch and how bad his breath smelled now.

"This is what your mother wanted you to listen to?" the woman asked.

"I hope not," said Megan.

"Who is this guy?" asked Sabrina.

"His name is Boom-boom Brogan," replied Megan. "He's kind of a jerk."

"All right, Boomers, it's time to take a trip in the rock 'n' roll time machine," said Boom-boom Brogan.

"Boomers?" said Connie.

"That's what he calls his listeners. You know, because his name is Boom-boom," said Megan. She rolled her eyes to show us what she thought of the name.

"Let's go back to the year 1967," said Boom-boom Brogan. He had a deep, friendly voice. "Lyndon Johnson was our president. Students at college campuses around the country were holding sit-ins to protest the Vietnam War. Riots were breaking out in the inner cities. You could buy a cup of coffee for a dime and a brand-new Ford Mustang for a thousand dollars."

Boom-boom Brogan's voice began to echo. It sounded as if he had just stepped into an echo chamber. "Okay, I've stepped into the rock 'n' roll time machine," he announced. "I'm closing the door and setting the dial for 1967. Now I'll just push this button here, and *awaaaaay we go!*"

There was a strange clanking noise, then a super-fast whizzing sound. Boom-boom Brogan frantically cried out:

"Something is wrong with the rock 'n' roll time machine! It won't stop! The years are speeding past—1967, 1966, 1965, 1964! Help, let me out of this thing!" It sounded as if he was banging on the walls with his fists.

"Now the dial's at 1945, 1943, 1942!" moaned Boom-boom Brogan. "What's going on? Now it's 1901, 1900, 1899! I never should have let the WBAZ-FM weatherman tune up the time machine. Now 1823, 1822, 1821!"

Finally, there was the sound of a big explosion on the radio. Then a hissing noise. This was followed by the chirping of birds.

"Where am I?" asked Boom-boom Brogan, between coughs. "Egads, the time machine dial says 1776! What am I doing here? Rock 'n' roll hasn't even been invented yet! Hey, I recognize this place! This is the town of New Elder! I'm on the village green! Look, there's the balm of Gilead tree! Look how young it looks! Gee, it doesn't look a day older than fifty! What's that noise? Sounds like snoring. Hey, who's the babe sleeping under the tree? Wait a sec, that's no babe! It's a guy with a wig! Why, it's *George Washington!*"

There was a loud yawn. "Where am I?" said a sleepy voice.

"You're on the village green in New Elder, Connecticut, George," said Boom-boom Brogan. "You fell asleep under the balm of Gilead tree."

"Who are you?" asked George Washington.

"I'm Boom-boom Brogan from WBAZ-FM. I'm from the year 2003. Want to hear something amazing? This balm of Gilead tree is still alive in my time."

"You're kidding me!" cried George Washington.

"No joke," said Boom-boom Brogan. "But now the town wants to chop it down."

"Hey, I may have chopped down a cherry tree," said George Washington, "but *I* would never chop down *this* tree."

"Don't worry, George. Four New Elder girls want to save the old balm of Gilead. They're raising money to buy a brace for the tree so it won't be cut down."

For a moment, we all just stared at each other, speechless.

Then Connie gasped.

Sabrina cried, "Oh, my gosh!"

I let out a shriek. Two shrieks!

"Oh, no!" groaned Megan.

"They're holding a sockathon!" continued Boom-boom Brogan.

"A *sockawhat?*" said George Washington.

Boom-boom Brogan explained what a sockathon was and how it worked. "We're asking all our WBAZ-FM listeners to donate socks and money. It's WBAZ-FM's Great Sockathon!"

"I'll be sure to tell Martha about it," said George Washington.

"Tell all your friends, George—Benjy Franklin, Johnny Adams, Tommy Jefferson."

"Hey, you'd be doing us all a favor if you take Tom Jefferson's stockings," said George Washington. *"Phew!"*

"Well, George, I have a show to get back to," said Boom-boom Brogan. "What's your favorite radio station?"

"WBAZ-FM!" cried George Washington. Then he asked, "What's a radio station?"

Boom-boom Brogan got back into his time machine and set the dial for 1967. This time he made it. He played a song called "Light My Fire."

My heart was thumping, I was so excited. And happy! I began whooping for joy. I couldn't resist. A man and a woman walking along the sidewalk turned and gave me the strangest looks.

"Are you the four sockathon girls?" the woman asked.

"That's us!" I exclaimed, proud as anything. I turned to Megan. She did not look happy. "And now thanks to Megan, we'll have no trouble getting socks!"

Megan groaned. "Yeah, now thanks to me, the whole world knows that I'm involved in the wackiest event of the century."

18 Sabrina

EVERYTHING changed after the sockathon was announced on the radio. It was amazing. Within hours after the broadcast, socks began pouring in. People in cars, SUVs, vans, and pickup trucks pulled into the Congregational church parking lot and got out with shopping bags stuffed with socks to drop off inside the church. Many of them waved or beeped their horns at us. A few people even came over and said hello and told us how glad they were that at least someone besides themselves cared about the old tree.

Connie's mother and little twin brothers and the Deitzes' big black Newfoundland dog showed up one morning with four plastic laundry baskets, one for each of us.

"I figured you could use them to carry socks," said Mrs. Deitz as she lifted them out of the Deitzes' green station wagon.

We loaded the laundry baskets up with socks and then lugged them from the church to the balm of Gilead tree. We dumped the socks out under the tree. Before long, we had a huge mountain of socks. We sat down in the tree's shade and got busy, stapling. We stapled one sock to another sock to another sock. We stapled and stapled and stapled. By the second week, the sock chain stretched all the way to Mechanic Street. Every afternoon while we stapled socks, we listened to Boom-boom Brogan on a boom box that Daisy brought from home.

Socks weren't the only things people donated—they also gave money. By the second week, we had raised $188.62. I put the money in a big manila envelope. On the front of the envelope, I wrote in big letters with a red marker:

SOCKATHON DONATIONS

I kept the envelope in my top bureau drawer, hidden under my socks and stockings.

In addition to socks and money, people also sent letters to the Congregational church that were addressed to the Sockathon Girls. In the letters, people related their memories of the tree. One woman told us how, years ago when she was little, she and her friends used Old Balmy as home base for hide-and-seek. A man wrote to us about the picnics he and his family used to have under the tree when he was a boy. We put the letters in a loose-leaf notebook. The funny thing was, the people who sent these letters didn't live in the WBAZ-FM listening area. They lived in places like Rockport, Maine, and Lubbock, Texas, and Boise, Idaho.

"How on earth did someone in Idaho find out about us?" I asked.

"Must've been from me," said Daisy proudly. "I told you, I've been going to chat rooms and telling people about the sockathon. Now we're mentioned on all these Web sites.

You should do a Google search on our sockathon. You wouldn't believe all the sites that mention us."

Here is one of the letters. It was written by a woman who lived in Erie, Pennsylvania.

Dear Sockathon Girls,

I commend all four of you on your endeavor to save the old balm of Gilead tree. I now live with my husband in Erie, Pennsylvania, but I grew up in New Elder. In 1974, we were married under the tree. I've enclosed a photograph of our wedding ceremony.

Best wishes,
Sara Armstrong

P.S. In July, we celebrate our thirtieth wedding anniversary. With that in mind, I am donating thirty socks and a check for thirty dollars.

The woman had enclosed a color snapshot. The color was washed out. The young bride and groom stood, smiling, in front of the balm of Gilead. A branch, lush with green leaves, was touching the man's shoulder. It looked as if the tree was patting the man on the shoulder.

We also began to receive something else—junk mail. Most of it came from nonprofit organizations asking us for donations. All sorts of charities sent letters: the American Cancer Society, the United Negro College Fund, Save Our Children, the American Red Cross, and the Alzheimer's Foundation. I had no clue why they sent us letters.

But Daisy did.

"I've been going to their Web sites and signing us up for more information," she said. "It was my mom's idea. She thought we might be able to learn something from them. She said we're kind of like a nonprofit organization asking for donations. I didn't realize, though, that they were going to ask *us* to donate money."

"What should we do with them?" I asked, holding up the charity letters. We were in the Sunday-school room, opening up that day's mail and sock donations. Denver was letting us use the Sunday-school room as our headquarters.

Megan snatched the letters out of my hand. "Here, I'll show you," she said.

She stepped over to the empty metal wastebasket that sat beside the teacher's desk and dropped them in. "There," she said. "See how easy that was."

But it wasn't easy. At least, not for me. The thing was, the letters were for such good causes. Plus, Daisy had given my name as the contact person. All the charity letters were addressed to me. Not Megan. Not Connie. Not Daisy. *Me.* I felt funny tossing them into the garbage.

We filled our laundry baskets up with socks. Then we slathered sunscreen all over our faces, necks, shoulders, arms, and legs. As we lugged the laundry baskets out of the church, I suddenly cried out: "Oops! I forgot my water bottle! I'll be right back."

I hadn't really forgotten my water bottle. I had left it on purpose in the Sunday-school room so I could have an excuse to return.

My water bottle was on the windowsill, sitting in the sun. I slipped it into my backpack. Then, quickly, I bent down and grabbed the letters that lay in the wastebasket. I stuffed them into my backpack, too, and hurried out of the room.

19 Megan

HAVE you ever had one of those days where everything seems to go wrong? Well, that was what my day was like. I'm talking about the day that Boom-boom Brogan announced the sockathon on the radio. I wanted the sockathon to die a quiet death so I could begin enjoying my summer vacation. Now, thanks to my mother, Boom-boom Brogan had told all his listeners to donate socks. Socks that I would have to staple!

I couldn't believe my mother! How could she use the sockathon as one of her WBAZ-FM promotions? How could she do such a thing to me?

"How could you do such a thing to me?" I said the moment she walked in the door that evening. I was sitting on the couch, watching TV.

Mom looked surprised. "What do you mean? I thought I was helping you."

"*Helping me?*" I cried. "I *hate* this stupid sockathon! I want it to end as soon as possible! Now, thanks to *you,* it'll drag on *all* summer!"

"What do you mean you hate it?"

"I hate it! It wasn't my idea to do this sockathon thing! It was Daisy's! I want to have fun this summer—not staple socks!"

"I'm sorry, Meg," said Mom. "I had no idea you felt this way. I thought you wanted to raise money to buy a brace for the balm of Gilead tree."

"Well, think again!" I told her.

Mom sat down beside me and placed her arm around me. She does that when she knows I'm upset. I slid out from under her arm and moved to the other end of the couch. I didn't want to be comforted.

Mom began to explain what had happened. "When I told Fred—my boss at WBAZ-FM—about the sockathon, he thought it was hysterical. I jokingly suggested we should do something on the sockathon. I swear, Meg, it was just a joke. But he loved the idea. It's the first idea of mine he has loved since he arrived at WBAZ-FM."

"That doesn't say much for him," I said.

Mom sighed. "I know you don't like this extra publicity, Meg, but, unfortunately, I don't know what I can do about it now."

I knew she felt bad. I also knew that, for the first time in weeks, she didn't look so tired and stressed out about her job. I could tell she was relieved that Fred had finally liked one of her marketing ideas.

"You should've asked me first," I said.

"You're right—I should've," said Mom.

"Well, I suppose it's not like it's the end of the world."

"I'm afraid I have more to tell you," said Mom.

"More?"

Mom nodded. "Boom-boom Brogan wants to do a live broadcast from the balm of Gilead tree."

"Excuse me?"

"He wants to interview you and your friends," said Mom.

"Oh, no!" I cried. I shook my head and waved my arms frantically back and forth. "No way, no how! Uh-uh! Sorry! Nope, not a chance! Don't even think about it! This sock-athon is a wacky idea! It's so uncool! So juvenile! I don't want the whole world to know I'm part of it! I refuse to give any interviews!"

Mom was quiet for a moment. She just looked at me. "Okay, I'll tell him," she said softly.

Now I felt bad. I knew this interview was important to her job.

"Oh, I guess it won't kill me if he interviews us," I said. "But you've got to promise you won't make any more suggestions at work without asking me, okay?"

"I promise," said Mom. Then she came over and gave me a little kiss on the top of my head.

20 Connie

ONE muggy morning in the second week of July, the four of us were sitting under the balm of Gilead tree, stapling socks, when Megan announced:

"Oh, by the way, the radio station my mom works for wants to do a live broadcast with us."

She said it so casually. So matter-of-factly. None of us believed her.

"You lie like a rug," teased Daisy.

"Fine, don't believe me," Megan said.

"Is this for real?" I asked.

"Yes, Connie, it's for real," sighed Megan.

"Boom-boom Brogan really wants to interview us?" asked Sabrina.

"Yes, he really wants to interview us," Megan said with a groan.

"We'll all be famous!" cried Daisy.

"Just what I want to be famous for," Megan grumbled.

The morning of the live radio broadcast, I was up at the crack of dawn, practically. I couldn't sleep. I was so nervous. The thought of being on the radio, with thousands of people listening, gave me butterflies in my stomach.

But that wasn't the only reason I couldn't sleep. I was also worried about Eliza Baker. I was worried that the live broadcast might upset her. I mean, it was going to take place right at the foot of the balm of Gilead tree. Her home. There was sure to be a lot of people. And noise. Would it scare her? Ever since Sabrina had heard her voice, I was hoping Eliza would make contact with us again. I was worried the live broadcast might keep that from ever happening.

I got dressed and went downstairs to the kitchen. I ate breakfast and then went outside to do my newspaper route. As I was stacking newspapers onto my little cart, Daisy appeared on her bike down the street. She was leaning over her handlebars and peddling furiously.

I stared at Daisy. I was shocked. She was all dressed up for the radio broadcast. Green shorts. A tie-dyed T-shirt. Red sneakers. Mismatched socks. But that wasn't what shocked me—it was her hair.

It had a wild, Day-Glo orange streak in it!

"Good, you're still here!" she cried as she whizzed into my driveway. She skidded to a stop right beside me. Now that she was closer, I saw she was also wearing rainbow glitter. It was sprinkled all about her eyes.

"I thought we were meeting at the church," I said.

That was the plan. Sabrina and I were to meet Daisy and Megan at the Congregational church at nine o'clock. Since Sabrina and I live on the same street, we were going to bicycle there together. We were to meet in front of my house at 8:30.

"I thought of the coolest idea last night," said Daisy as she hopped off her bike. She slipped off her backpack. Unzipping it, she reached in and pulled out a bunch of computer printouts. They were held together by a big green paper clip. She handed me one of the printouts. It was a flyer that she had created on the computer. There was a headline and text. The headline screamed:

Save Old Balmy!
Donate to the Great Sockathon!

"So what do you think?" asked Daisy. "I thought we could put one in each of your newspapers. I figured we should ask people to donate while we're getting all this free publicity."

"We can't do this, Daisy," I said. I handed the flyer back to her.

Daisy looked crestfallen. "Why not?"

"Because we can't," I said. "It'll only get me into trouble. It's an advertisement. People pay money to put things like this in the newspaper. We can't just stick it in without paying. What if the newspaper finds out?"

"The newspaper will never find out," said Daisy.

"Don't be so sure," I said.

"Who would tell?"

"Try Mrs. Campbell."

Daisy didn't argue. "Tell you what," she said. "We won't put a flyer in Mrs. Campbell's newspaper. How about that?"

"I don't know," I said.

"Oh, come on," said Daisy. "Don't be such a scaredy-cat."

"I'm not a scaredy-cat!" I said.

"You sure sound like one."

"Oh, all right, we'll do it!" I said. "But I better not get into trouble."

"Don't worry, Connie, you won't get in trouble."

Daisy stuck a flyer in every newspaper except one. "This'll be Mrs. Campbell's," she said. "Which I will personally carry." She tucked it under her arm.

"*I'll* carry it," I said.

Daisy looked hurt that I didn't trust her. "Okay," she said, and handed me the newspaper.

Daisy and I set off down the sidewalk. When we got to Mrs. Campbell's house, Daisy said, "Don't look now, but the old bat is on her porch."

"Oh, brother!" I groaned. I couldn't believe it. What was Mrs. Campbell doing out on her porch so early in the morning?

I grabbed another newspaper from my cart to give to the Butterworths. They lived in the house next to Mrs. Campbell's. I figured I'd cut across Mrs. Campbell's driveway to their driveway. Save myself some steps.

"Don't worry, I'll protect you," whispered Daisy as she followed me up onto Mrs. Campbell's porch.

"Hello, Mrs. Campbell," I said. Very cheerfully. "Here's

your newspaper—bright and early." I gave her my friend-liest, most polite smile.

Mrs. Campbell peered first at me, then at Daisy.

"Good lord!" she gasped, horrified. She pointed the end of her cane at the orange streak in Daisy's hair. "What on earth have you done to your head?"

Daisy looked worried. She touched her hair. "What's wrong? Did I mess it up?"

"When I was growing up, a girl would never do such a thing to her hair," said Mrs. Campbell. "And if she did, she'd hear about it from her mother—good and loud!"

I'd heard enough. I just wanted to get away. As fast as possible. I gave Mrs. Campbell her newspaper and said, "Well, see you later, Mrs. Campbell."

I took off like a flash down the porch stairs.

"God, I feel so, so sorry for you!" said Daisy as she hurried to catch up with me. She said it in a very loud voice. "I don't know how you put up with her every day!"

"*Shh!*" I whispered. "She'll hear you!"

"That's the idea!" Daisy whispered back.

Then suddenly Daisy stopped. Gasped. "Oh, no!"

I turned and looked at her. "What's the matter?"

"I think you gave Mrs. Campbell the newspaper with a flyer in it," said Daisy. "You were holding it under your left arm, and that's the newspaper you gave her."

I quickly opened the newspaper I was holding. There was no flyer. "Oh, *no!*" I blurted. "I just wanted to get out as fast as possible. I wasn't paying attention."

"We'll have to go back and get it," said Daisy.

We turned toward Mrs. Campbell's porch. Too late. Mrs. Campbell had already opened up her newspaper. She was holding it in front of her face.

"This is all your fault!" I said, glaring at Daisy.

"*My* fault?"

"Yes, *your* fault!"

"But *you're* the one who gave her the newspaper," said Daisy.

"Yeah, but you're the genius who thought of sticking flyers in the newspapers!" I threw my hands up in the air. "Well, there goes my job!"

"What are you talking about?" said Daisy. "You're not going to lose your job. I bet Mrs. Campbell never even notices the flyer." She placed her arm around me and flashed me a big smile. I got a great view of her bright green braces. "Now c'mon, cheer up! We have a live radio broadcast to do!"

21 Daisy

THE highlight of the summer—at least for me—was the day that Boom-boom Brogan came to the village green and did his live radio broadcast.

The day didn't start out well. Not at all. First, Connie gave me a hard time about my sockathon flyers. She didn't want to put them in her newspapers. Then Mrs. Campbell gave me a hard time about my hair. Things got better, though, when we got to the village green.

I had a blast. It was a day full of surprises. The first surprise was Megan. She actually paid me a compliment about the orange streak in my hair.

"Go for it, girl!" she said, grinning.

The second surprise was Boom-boom Brogan. Ever since he had announced the sockathon on the radio, we'd been listening to his show every afternoon. I brought a boom box so we could listen while we stapled socks. From the sound of his voice, I thought he was going to be this real hunk.

Not so.

He turned out to be this big, overweight, furry-looking guy who was around sixty years old. He had long shaggy hair that was mostly gray and a goatee. He also wore granny glasses with lenses that were tinted a rosy purple.

Another thing that surprised me was how little it takes to do a live radio broadcast. I was expecting it to be like a movie set, with lots of people running around and big stage lights, cameras, and a director shouting "Action!"

But there was just a white van parked at the village green that said WBAZ-FM—THE BEST OF THE '60S, '70S AND '80S—on each side. A long folding table had been set up beside the balm of Gilead tree. When we arrived, a technician was setting up two microphones at the table. The mikes were attached to wires that ran across the lawn and disappeared into the van.

The entire broadcast took place on the village green, beside the balm of Gilead tree. A huge crowd had gathered to watch. For days Boom-boom Brogan had been promoting the event on his show. Denver was there. So was my family and Sabrina's and Connie's parents. And, of course, Megan's mother. She was running around, looking very stressed.

At 2:00 p.m., *The Boom-boom Brogan Show* began. "Today we are broadcasting live from the village green in New Elder," said Boom-boom Brogan in his deep, velvety voice. "I'm standing right beside the huge balm of Gilead tree. I gotta tell you, Boomers, this tree is awesome. It's about two hundred and seventy-five years old, yet it looks better than I do."

People in the crowd laughed.

"I have with me four very special guests," he continued, strolling over to where Megan's mother had instructed us to stand. "They're the four girls who are making a sock chain to raise money to buy a brace for the balm of Gilead tree. Yes, I'm with the one and only Sockathon Girls! Let's hear it for the Sockathon Girls!"

The crowd applauded and cheered. I bowed to everyone—which got quite a few laughs from the audience.

Boom-boom Brogan had each of us introduce ourselves. Connie got really nervous when it was her turn. She couldn't speak. Lowering her head, she said her name so softly nobody heard her.

"I'm sorry, dear, what was that?" asked Boom-boom Brogan.

"Connie," she repeated in a mousy voice.

Boom-boom Brogan, smiling, patted Connie on the shoulder to make her feel more at ease. Then he said to Megan, "So, Megan, baby, tell me—whose idea was it to do this sockathon?"

Megan pointed at me and said, *"Hers!"*

Boom-boom Brogan came over to me and said, "So you're the brains behind this operation, eh, Daisy?"

"That's me, Boom-boom!" I said.

Boom-boom Brogan smiled at me. His eyes gleamed behind his tinted granny glasses. "I understand a brace costs six thousand dollars," he said. "You really think you'll be able to raise that much money?"

"Hey, ya gotta believe!" I said. I glanced over at Denver. He gave me a big thumbs-up.

"For all of you who are listening, I've got to tell you this is one long sock chain," said Boom-boom Brogan. "It stretches all the way from the balm of Gilead tree to the other end of the village green. Then it begins again on the other side of Main Street."

"And then it goes down Chestnut Street, then Mechanic Street, then State Street, then Willow Street!" I said.

Boom-boom Brogan whistled in amazement. "What are you kids trying to do? Get in *The Guinness Book of World Records*?"

We all laughed.

Then Boom-boom Brogan said, "Well, girls, what do you say we take a trip in the rock 'n' roll time machine?"

A short, bald man in baggy Bermuda shorts and a bright, flowery Hawaiian shirt stood behind the table that had been set up by the tree. The top of the table was covered with all sorts of things that he could make sounds with—coconut shells, a baby rattle, a pair of old shoes, a bathroom plunger, whistles, pots, a washboard, a wooden spoon, bells, even a chain. He was, Mrs. Geherty had told us, the sound-effects man. Usually, WBAZ-FM used recorded sound effects. But that day, for the benefit of the crowd on hand, there was a sound-effects man to make noises.

The sound-effects man had his own microphone. He

leaned into it and, using only his mouth, made the sound of a door creaking open. Then, using two coconut shell halves, he made the sound of a door closing with a slam.

Speaking into his microphone, Boom-boom Brogan said, "I'm setting the dial for the year 1965."

The sound-effects man made a lot of funny noises with his mouth. If you were listening on the radio, you would have sworn it was a time machine taking off. Or a kitchen blender that had just been switched on.

Suddenly, several women in the audience screamed. The crowd parted, and out walked four guys with shaggy hair, dressed in tight-fitting matching gray suits.

"It's the Beatles!" cried Boom-boom Brogan.

They were, of course, just four guys dressed to look like the Beatles. Smiling, the fake Beatles walked over to us and stopped. "Hey there, Sockathon Girls," said one of them. He had some kind of British accent. "I'm John Lennon!"

"Hey, John!" I said.

At Boom-boom Brogan's request, the look-alike Beatles sang a song called "Help!" "Help! I need somebody . . ."

"And now," said Boom-boom Brogan when they'd finished the song, "I'd like to *help* you girls by making a small donation to your sockathon."

He reached into his pocket and pulled out a green sock that had little guitars and musical notes stitched all over it.

"This is my favorite sock," said Boom-boom Brogan. He pretended to be sad at having to part with it. He dabbed his eyes with a handkerchief.

I pretended that his sock smelled bad. "Peee-yew!" I cried, holding my nose.

The crowd loved it. Laughing, they clapped and clapped.

"She's right, Boom-boom," said the look-alike Paul McCartney, speaking with the same accent. "I can smell it from here! Whew!"

Everybody was laughing. Even Boom-boom Brogan. I smiled and waved to the crowd.

Hey, what can I say? A star was born!

22 Sabrina

TALK about amazing! After we did our live broadcast, we were flooded with even more socks. It was totally awesome! We got bags and bags of socks. People dropped them off at the Congregational church. Socks also came by mail. One person even sent a FedEx envelope with socks in it!

And Daisy was pretty amazing, too. Who knew she'd be so good on the radio! We all congratulated her after the show was over. Even Boom-boom Brogan gave her a big hug.

The sock chain grew and grew. It stretched all the way from the old balm of Gilead tree on the village green to the playground at the New Elder Elementary School over on Schoolhouse Road. It ran along Chestnut Street, then down Mechanic Street, then State Street, Willow Street, Arch Street, Lewis Avenue, Valley Drive, and Shore Road.

For the most part, people were very supportive. But not everyone was. Some store owners told us they didn't want the sock chain running in front of their stores. They were afraid customers might trip over it. So we moved it. We had promised Mrs. Sargent we wouldn't cause any trouble.

Once a week, Mrs. Sargent came by to visit us and see

how we were doing. She was always amazed by how much the sock chain had grown since her last visit.

Socks weren't the only things that poured in after the live radio broadcast. So did money. By the end of July, we had raised $983.75. The live radio broadcast alone brought in more than $550.

I was in charge of holding all the cash and checks. I put them—as well as all the letters and junk mail we got—in a manila envelope that I kept in my top bureau drawer. This worked out fine until one afternoon my mother discovered the envelope while she was putting away some of my clean clothes.

"What's this, Sabrina?" she asked from the top of the stairs.

"What's what?" I asked on my way up to my bedroom. I had just come home from a long day of stapling socks.

"This," she said, holding up the envelope. It was bulging with money and checks and letters.

"That's mine!" I said. I went over and snatched it out of her hand.

"I know it's yours," she said. "I found it when I was putting away your socks. This isn't money from your sockathon, is it?"

She knew perfectly well it was. The words SOCKATHON DONATIONS were lettered right across the front of the envelope.

"That's what it says, doesn't it?" I replied.

"Don't be snide," my mother said. "You shouldn't keep it in your dresser. What if something were to happen to it? If it were me, I'd put the money in the bank."

Much as I hated to admit it, I knew my mother was right.

"The bank stays open late this evening. If you'd like, I'll drive you over there."

So that's what we did. While my mother sat nearby in the bank's waiting area, leafing through a magazine, I sat with a bank officer and opened a savings account. My mother thought it was important that I do it by myself. But it wasn't really by myself. As it turned out, my mother had to show two forms of identification (she showed her driver's license and a credit card). She and I also had to sign something called a signature card. That meant I could take money out of the account all by myself.

"How would you like your name to appear on the account?" the man asked, gazing at me over his glasses.

"What do you mean?" I asked.

"Well, would you like your full name on it, your first and last name with your middle initial, or just your first and last names?"

"Sabrina Martha Ingalls," I said.

The man asked me other questions. What was my date of birth? What was my mailing address and telephone number? What was my Social Security number? He typed all my answers into a computer.

The bank officer reached into a desk drawer and pulled out a small blue booklet. He entered my name in it and then turned to me.

"This is your savings account passbook," he said, holding the booklet open to the first page. "And this is your savings account number." He tapped his index finger on a long number beside my name. Then he took out a few small, rectangular slips from his drawer. Some of the slips were green, some pink.

"And these are deposit slips and withdrawal slips," he explained.

He showed me how to fill out a deposit slip (they were the green slips) and a withdrawal slip (the pink ones). Then he told me other things about the account. Things I didn't see why I needed to know. Like how to get a cashier's check.

"Why would I want a cashier's check?" I asked.

"In case you want to send money through the mail," he explained. "Now, how much would you like to deposit into your savings account today?"

I reached down and picked up the brown envelope that was sitting on my lap. It was as stuffed as a pillow with money and checks. I undid the clasp and dumped everything out onto the desk.

"Nine hundred and eighty-three dollars and seventy-five cents—altogether," I said.

The bank officer stared at the pile, then at me, with a startled look on his face. He whistled in amazement.

"Wow! That's a pretty impressive amount," he said as he separated the cash from the checks. When he'd finished, he had me fill out a deposit slip, listing the cash and checks separately. Then he had me come with him up to the teller's window.

"This is Sabrina," the bank officer said to a red-haired woman at the teller's window. "Sabrina, this is Mrs. Adams."

"Hello," said the woman, smiling.

"Whenever you make a deposit or withdrawal transaction, or if you ever need a cashier's check, you do it here at the teller's window," the bank officer said to me as he handed Mrs. Adams the deposits and the savings account passbook. After Mrs. Adams had processed everything, she handed me back my passbook.

It was kind of scary, in a way, being at the teller's window. It seemed so . . . so grown-up.

On the car ride home, I flipped open my savings account passbook to the first page. Printed up at the top, in black type, was the amount that was in the savings account: $983.75.

"Now the money is safe," said my mother, smiling, as she glanced at me through the rearview mirror.

Although I knew the money wasn't really mine, I wanted to tell my mother how grown-up and responsible it made me feel to have my very own savings account.

But I couldn't. Not to my mother.

23 Megan

IT'S funny. I know I was the one who didn't want to do the sockathon, but I found I kind of liked all the attention we got from it. I know we weren't really famous or anything, but I still felt like a big celebrity. I began thinking like one, too. Whenever Mom asked me to do something, I'd ask myself if a celebrity would do this. One thing I was pretty sure a celebrity did not have to do was visit her tiny, old, shriveled-up great-great-aunt every Tuesday evening.

A week after the radio broadcast, Mom and I went to visit Great-aunt Carrie at the nursing home. When we got there, Great-aunt Carrie was, as usual, in her bedroom with her nightgown on. She was curled up in bed with her back to the door. Her blinds were lowered—they were always lowered—so it was sort of hard to make her out in the weak light.

"She's sleeping," I whispered to Mom. "Let's not disturb her."

Mom gave me a look. I smiled.

Mom turned on the lamp that was on the table beside Great-aunt Carrie's bed. Then she pulled up a chair beside

Great-aunt Carrie and sat down. I went over and plopped down in the green armchair that was in the corner of the room.

"Hi, Aunt Carrie," Mom said as she gently stroked Great-aunt Carrie's skeletonlike hand. "It's me, Ellen. Megan and I are here to visit with you."

Great-aunt Carrie turned and peered at Mom. She didn't say a word. She just stared. A hard, piercing stare.

Another fun visit, I said to myself. Bored, I took out my cell phone and began to play a game, but I knew Mom would get mad. So I just sat there and fiddled with it—pulling the antenna up and down, touching the keypad.

For the next fifteen minutes, I sat there while Mom had her one-sided conversation with Great-aunt Carrie. I was bored out of my mind. Finally I said, "Can we go now?"

Mom looked at me. She was ready to go, too. I could tell.

"Well, Aunt Carrie, Megan and I have to say good-bye now. We'll see you next Tuesday."

Mom leaned over, and I quickly looked away. But not quick enough. I saw Mom give Great-aunt Carrie a kiss on her cheek. The thought of kissing that old, wrinkly skin totally grossed me out.

I walked out of the room. I was heading down the hallway when an old, skinny guy in a blue bathrobe shuffled out from one of the rooms. He was a real mess. Unshaven face. Scruffy-looking white hair. Baggy old pajamas. Grungy slippers. Glasses with big, ugly black frames.

The man's face lit up. "Lucy!" he cried.

I thought he was talking to somebody behind me. But nobody was there. Not even Mom. She was way down the hall by Great-aunt Carrie's room, chatting with a nurse.

"I've been waiting for you, Lucy," he said, shuffling toward me.

"I'm not Lucy," I told him.

"Where have you been?" Now he sounded annoyed.

I tried to ignore him. I went to walk past him, but he stood right in my way.

"Where are you going?" he asked, with a frantic look in his eyes. He grabbed me by the arm.

"Hey!" I cried, yanking my arm away. I slipped past him and began to run—fast.

"Don't go, Lucy!" he called after me. "Don't leave me here! Please don't!"

My heart was thumping, I was so upset. When I got outside, I ran onto the front lawn and flopped down on the grass.

"Where were you?" I yelled at my mother when she finally stepped out of the building. "Did you see what that guy just did to me?"

"No, what happened?" asked Mom.

"You didn't see it?" I cried. "This old guy tried to attack me! He called me Lucy!"

"I'm sure he wouldn't have hurt you," Mom said. "The poor man probably has Alzheimer's. He was probably just confused."

I stared at my mother. I couldn't believe her. How could she side with that old guy? I felt tears in my eyes. The next thing I knew, I was crying.

"I hate this place!" I said, wiping away a tear with the back of my hand. "I'm never coming back here! Never! *Never!* So don't ask me!"

Mom looked like she was about to argue with me, but she didn't. Instead, she just sighed, aimed her key chain at our Jeep, and opened the doors. As Mom drove out of the nursing-home parking lot, she glanced over at me seated beside her.

"All right, Megan," she said. "I won't ask you to come here again."

Neither of us spoke on the ride home. I just looked out my window. I was still really mad at Mom. We drove through town. As we drove past the village green, I wanted to glance over at our sock chain. But I didn't—it was on Mom's side of the street. We passed the Congregational church (the balm of Gilead was also on Mom's side) and then the church cemetery. We passed the small headstone that I had found the day we discovered Eliza Baker's grave. Back then, the grave had purple lilacs on it. Today it had orange day lilies. I stretched my neck to see if I could spot Eliza Baker's grave.

But I couldn't. There were too many other graves in the way.

24 Connie

FOR weeks after the live radio broadcast, people kept dropping off tons of socks. This kept us very busy. Well, it kept three of us very busy. In late July, Daisy and her family had gone off on vacation to Cape Cod for about a week. When Daisy returned, she brought us back a present: an old, faded pink sock. She found it, she said, washed up on the beach.

By the first week in August, we had stapled more than two miles of socks and collected over $1,100. The sock chain now stretched all the way from the village green to the football and soccer fields at the New Elder Middle School that was on Maple Street. Every day we stapled socks under the balm of Gilead tree. After we were finished stapling, we took the new string of socks and carried it, by bike, to the end of the sock chain. Then we attached the new section of socks.

I hadn't seen Mrs. Campbell for twenty-two straight days. In fact, the last time I had seen her was that day Daisy placed that flyer about our sockathon in her newspaper. After all this time, I figured I was safe: Mrs. Campbell had not seen Daisy's flyer. If she had, I surely would have heard about it.

While I was glad about that, I was worried about something else: Eliza Baker. It had been over six weeks since she had spoken to Sabrina. Day after day after day, we sat under the balm of Gilead tree, stapling socks. In all that time, I thought Eliza would try to make contact with us. But she didn't. Not once.

And I thought I knew why, too: the live radio broadcast. I was sure it had scared her. I didn't tell Sabrina, Megan, or Daisy this, though. For one thing, they were so swept up in the sockathon, they hardly ever mentioned Eliza anymore. The other reason I didn't say anything was that I was worried about what they might say: that I was taking Eliza Baker way too seriously. Maybe I was. But I felt Eliza and I had a special connection. So I just kept quiet. And waited. And hoped.

And then one August day I decided to *do* something. If Eliza Baker wasn't going to make contact with us, *I'd* make contact with her. I'd leave her something. Candy! Eliza Baker was a kid, after all. What kid didn't like candy? So I left her a Baby Ruth candy bar. I hid it between two roots of the balm of Gilead tree, just below the spot where she and her friend, Ginny, had carved "Friends to the End." I figured if I left something like Nerds or Snickers or some other candy that wasn't around when Eliza Baker was alive, she might not know what it was. I knew Baby Ruths had been around in the 1930s.

One morning we spent nearly two hours lugging laundry baskets filled with socks from the church to the balm of Gilead tree. Even after all that, there were still socks back at the church. Sabrina and Megan went to go get them while Daisy and I got busy stapling socks. Before I sat down, I stepped over to the trunk of the balm of Gilead to check the Baby Ruth bar.

It was gone!

"Oh, my gosh!" I blurted out. "Daisy, you won't believe this, but I left out a candy bar and now it's gone! It was right here between these two roots!"

"*You* put that Baby Ruth there?" said Daisy.

"You knew about it?" I asked, surprised.

"I ate it," replied Daisy.

"*You* ate it!"

"I didn't know it was yours," she said. "Sorry!"

I couldn't believe Daisy. I was so mad at her. How could she eat Eliza's candy bar? To show her just how mad I was, I let out a big, loud I-can't-believe-you sigh. Then I spun around and marched across the village green toward the church.

"Hey, I said I was sorry!" Daisy called out after me. "Gee whiz!"

I crossed Elm Street and stomped up the front steps of the church. I was about to go into the church when, suddenly, back at the village green, I heard a shriek. I whirled around. Daisy was standing by the balm of Gilead tree with her head tilted back, staring up at the leafy branches.

I dashed back to the tree. "What's wrong?"

Daisy was so excited, she couldn't speak. She just stared at me, gasping. It was scary. It was like she was having an asthma attack.

"Breathe, Daisy!" I cried.

"Eliza Baker—she—she just spoke to me!" cried Daisy.

25 Daisy

CONNIE tells me I let out a loud scream after I heard Eliza Baker's ghost. But I don't remember screaming. I'm not saying I didn't scream. I just don't remember doing it. I do remember one thing, though. Connie's face. She looked so envious when I told her what had happened.

"She *spoke* to you?" she said, her eyes wide.

I nodded. I could scarcely speak. My heart was racing a million miles per hour.

"I can't believe she spoke to you and not me!" said Connie. She sounded hurt. "I'm the one who left her a candy bar! What did she say?"

"What did *who* say?" I heard a voice behind me ask.

It was Megan. She and Sabrina had returned with more socks. Each of them were lugging plastic laundry baskets, heaped high with socks.

"Eliza spoke to Daisy!" said Connie.

Sabrina stared at me. "She did?" She put down her basket and came over to me. "What did she say, Daisy?"

Megan and Connie stepped closer, too.

"She said, 'Don't give up,'" I replied.

Megan frowned. "'Don't give up'?"

I nodded.

"Well, that makes sense!" said Connie. "First she asked Sabrina to help her, right? Now she's asked Daisy not to give up. She knows the balm of Gilead tree is rotting and that we're trying to save the tree."

"Oh, sure, that must be it!" Megan said sarcastically.

I turned to Megan. "You don't believe she spoke to me, do you?"

"Come on, Daisy, a tree can't talk."

"It's not the tree, Megan," I said. "It's *Eliza*."

"Oh, excuse me!" said Megan. "Eliza!"

"I'd be careful what you say around this tree," Connie warned her.

Megan put her hand to her mouth, pretending to be worried. "Oh, my gosh, I forgot: Eliza might be listening!"

"You know what your problem is, Megan?" I said. "You don't believe."

"Believe in what? Ghosts? Well, you're right: I don't."

"No, it's more than that!" I said. "You don't believe that the impossible can happen! You don't believe that something mysterious, something that can't be explained, something magical, something miraculous, something wonderful can really happen! You don't believe that our sockathon will raise much money or that we'll be able to save Old Balmy! Why, you don't even believe in Tug McGraw's saying, 'Ya gotta believe.' That's why Eliza will never speak to you!"

Megan just shrugged her shoulders and said, "Whatever!"

26 Sabrina

I WAS so relieved when Daisy heard Eliza Baker's voice. While I didn't dare tell my friends this, I had begun to wonder if maybe Megan had been right—maybe I had imagined the entire thing. Now that Daisy had heard the voice, too, I knew I really *had* heard Eliza Baker.

We quit early that day. It had nothing to do with Daisy hearing Eliza, though. We quit because it was so unbelievably hot and humid. The whole Northeast was in the middle of a sizzling heat wave. It reached ninety-eight degrees that afternoon. And it also hadn't rained in weeks. The grass on the village green looked as dry as shredded wheat.

When I got home, my mother hadn't picked up the mail yet. The black metal mailbox on our front porch was crammed with letters and magazines. I gathered them up and stepped inside. Looking through the mail, I saw I had received a letter. I stared at it in disbelief. It was a letter from a charity!

"Oh, no!" I groaned. How did they get my home address? Then I realized how. . . .

Daisy!

Ever since Daisy had given out my name, I had received dozens of letters from charities. But the letters had all come to the church, not to my house. Now Daisy must have given out my home address! The charities all wanted the same thing: money. Today's letter was asking for money to help kids with cystic fibrosis, a genetic disease that affects some 30,000 children in the United States. Many of the kids will not even live to reach adulthood, the letter said, and asked me to be as generous as possible.

I put the letter down, but I couldn't put those kids out of my mind. I felt bad that many of them would not get to live to be adults. In a way, they were kind of like Eliza Baker. But I had no money to give them. Then I realized I did have money—our sockathon money.

I kept the savings account passbook upstairs in my bedroom, in the top drawer of my bureau. I never touched it except when I went to deposit money into the account. (Since opening the account, I had made five deposits.)

I went into my bedroom, closed the door, and got out my passbook. I opened it to the page where I had stuck in all the deposit and withdrawal slips. I picked out a pink withdrawal slip and examined it. I had never really looked at it closely before. It said:

Date: _____

Savings Account Number: _____

Amount of Withdrawal: _____

And then a line for my signature.

I wrote out the date and my savings account number. When I got to the dollar amount, I paused. The charity letter had asked me to be as generous as possible. The reply card had listed several boxes with dollar amounts beside each box: $25, $75, $100, $500. What did they consider generous? Well, $25 seemed pretty generous to me. I checked the $25 box. But then I thought, *No, that can't be generous. If that was generous, why would other—higher—amounts be listed?* So I crossed out the $25 box and checked the $75 box. Then I wrote the same amount on the withdrawal slip.

And then I signed my name.

I wasn't at all nervous about filling out a withdrawal slip. In fact, to be honest, I felt like a little kid playing grown-up. I stuck the charity's reply card into the postage-paid return envelope and then stuck the envelope and the withdrawal slip into my savings account passbook. I put the passbook under my shirt and went downstairs.

"Where are you going?" my mother called from the kitchen when she heard me open the front door.

"I'm just going out for a little walk," I replied. "I'll be right back."

Quickly, before my mother could ask me another question, I stepped outside and walked as fast as I could into town, which was where my bank branch was located.

Hardly anyone was in the bank when I got there. The bank officer who had helped me open the savings account wasn't there. Nor was Mrs. Adams, the bank teller. I didn't even have to wait in line. I just went right up to the teller window, handed the woman my withdrawal slip and passbook, and said, "I'd like a cashier's check, please."

I expected the teller to ask me why I wanted one, but she didn't. She just said, "Who would you like it made out to, dear?"

"The Cystic Fibrosis Foundation," I replied.

A minute later, the teller handed me back my passbook and a cashier's check for seventy-five dollars. It couldn't have been easier.

I inserted the cashier's check into the charity's return envelope and sealed it. Stepping outside, I saw a mailbox just down the street. I hurried over to it and dropped the envelope in.

On my way home, I kept thinking about the cashier's check. I kept thinking about the seventy-five dollars that I given away.

Seventy-five dollars that wasn't mine.

All of a sudden I wanted my check back. I wanted to race back to the bank and return the money I had withdrawn. But how could I? The cashier's check was sitting, out of reach, in the mailbox.

"Have a nice walk?" my mother asked from the kitchen when I stepped into the house.

"Uh, yeah, I guess so," I replied.

"You guess so?"

"No, I did."

What else could I say? I couldn't tell my mother that I had just given away seventy-five dollars of the money that Megan, Daisy, Connie, and I had worked so hard to raise so we could buy a brace for the balm of Gilead tree. I didn't want her to know I couldn't be trusted with a savings account.

All summer long, I had shown my mother how responsible I was. Now I had blown it.

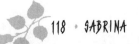

27 Megan

I'LL never forget that week in August. For one thing, it was wicked hot. For seven straight days, the temperature soared above ninety degrees. The weather guy on WBAZ-FM kept saying the heat wave would break in a few days, but it didn't. It was just one broiling-hot, global-warming day after another.

There's another reason, though, why I won't forget that week: we held a séance one evening.

It was Connie's idea. She was hoping Eliza would communicate with us during the séance. That's what you do in a séance—you try to communicate with the dead.

We held the séance one Thursday evening after the sun had set, just as it was growing dark. There was a pinkish glow in the sky where the sun had gone down behind the flat-roofed buildings on Elm Street. To do the séance, Connie had brought some little, fat candles and a barbecue fire-starter pistol. She placed the candles under the balm of Gilead, near our pile of socks, and then lit the candles.

"So now what do we do?" I asked.

"We sit down and hold hands," said Connie.

We sat down, cross-legged, and formed a circle around the burning candles. We reached out and held one another's hands.

"Now what?" asked Daisy.

"We close our eyes," said Connie.

"Okay, my eyes are closed," I said.

"Now concentrate on Eliza," said Connie.

"Okay, I'm concentrating," I replied.

"Eliza," said Connie, speaking in a loud voice. I guess she thought she had to speak loudly in order to communicate with the dead. "It's us, Eliza—your friends, Sabrina, Daisy, Megan, and me, Connie. Can you hear us?"

We sat in silence, listening. Crickets chirped in the grass. Somewhere above, in the balm of Gilead leaves, a cicada buzzed.

"Can you hear us, Eliza?" Connie asked again.

Then a ghostly voice replied: "Yeeesss, I-I-I can!"

It was only me, having some fun.

Daisy thought it was Sabrina. "Will you stop it, Sabrina!" she said.

"What? That wasn't me!" said Sabrina.

I opened my eyes. Daisy, Sabrina, and Connie were glaring at me. "Sorry, I couldn't resist," I said, smiling.

"Try again," Sabrina said to Connie.

We closed our eyes again. "Eliza, if you're here, please make your presence known to us."

We all sat perfectly quiet, waiting for Eliza to make her presence known.

I began to giggle. I couldn't help it.

"Shh!" hushed Daisy, squeezing my hand.

Connie tried several more times to get Eliza to communicate, but she didn't. Finally, we gave up.

"Well, we tried," said Sabrina.

"Maybe she's too high up in the tree to hear us," said Daisy. She lifted her eyes toward the leafy branches that covered us like a huge umbrella.

"Look!" she gasped, pointing upward.

A short string of socks was dangling from one of the lower branches.

"Oh, my gosh!" said Connie. "Eliza must have put them there!"

"Nice try, guys," I said, "but I'm not falling for it."

Sabrina looked at me. "What are you talking about?"

"You know what I'm talking about," I said. "You guys put those socks up in the tree before we did the séance to make me believe in Eliza."

"We didn't put those socks up there!" cried Daisy.

"Oh, yeah, uh-huh," I said.

"We didn't!" insisted Connie.

Sabrina gazed up at the string of socks. "We can't leave those socks up there. You know what Mrs. Sargent said. We can't leave any socks lying around."

"There's only one way to get them down," said Daisy. "One of us is going to have to climb up and get them."

"Maybe we should bring a rake tomorrow and pull them down," suggested Sabrina.

"Scared to climb the tree, are we?" I said. "Face it—you guys are scared stiff of Eliza Baker."

And then the most unexpected thing happened. Connie stepped forward and said, "I'll climb up the tree."

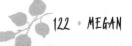

28 Connie

AFTER I said I'd climb up the balm of Gilead tree, Megan laughed. She thought I was kidding. But I wasn't kidding. I was perfectly serious. I was scared to death, but I was dead serious. I had something to prove.

"I will! I'll climb up and get them!" I said.

I grabbed one of the lower branches that curved skyward from the huge trunk. I hoisted myself up and grabbed the branch just above it.

"Connie, what are you doing?" asked Daisy, alarmed.

"What does it look like I'm doing?" I replied. "I'm climbing the tree to get the socks. You all think I'm the biggest chicken on earth."

"Nobody thinks that," said Sabrina.

"You do so! You all do!"

"Connie, you don't have to do this," said Megan.

Oh, yes, I do, I thought. I had to prove I wasn't a big chicken.

I tried not to show it, but I was terrified. I hate heights. I'm also not very athletic. As I climbed, I made sure not to look down. I know I probably wasn't very high up, but it sure felt like I was. The higher I got, the slower I climbed.

I must've been about fifteen feet up in the tree when a horrible thought occurred to me:

Is this the branch Eliza Baker fell from?

And then I felt it. It was the eeriest feeling.

Someone was on the branch beside me!

"Oh, God!" I murmured.

I thought my heart would explode, it was pounding so fast. I slowly glanced over.

A girl in a dirty, torn white dress was sitting on the branch beside me. She had honey-colored hair, bouncy curls, and the most sickly-looking pale skin. There was a big gash on her cheek, and her face was covered with black-and-blue marks.

It was the girl from the newspaper photograph.

Eliza Baker!

I know I'd been hoping that Eliza would speak to me, but this was much more than I had bargained for. The worst part was, I couldn't run away. I was stuck in the tree. I shut my eyes, hoping, wishing, praying that she would disappear. When I opened my eyes, she was still there. I was shaking all over. I was causing the branch to shake.

"Hey, you okay up there?" I heard Megan call from below.

I glanced down. Megan, Sabrina, and Daisy stood at the bottom of the tree, with their heads tilted back, staring up at me. I tried to call to them. But no words came out of my mouth. Not even a squeak.

I turned and looked at Eliza.

"Oh, don't be such an old lady!" she said. "I'm not going to hurt you!"

I didn't say anything. I couldn't. I was too scared. She started to come toward me. Her face was nearly touching mine!

Startled, I jerked backward. As I did, I lost my balance. My right hand slipped from the branch that I was holding onto. I tried to grab another branch. I missed.

The next thing I knew, I was plunging through the branches.

29 Daisy

CONNIE!"

I screamed it at the top of my lungs as I saw her fall
out of the balm of Gilead tree. I still shudder when I think
about it.

The whole thing happened so quickly. Connie was cau-
tiously making her way up the tree when she stopped. She
just sat there for a moment. Then she let out this loud, horrible scream and tumbled out of the tree.

She was very lucky: she wasn't that high up, and she
landed right on top of the pile of socks. I hate to think what
would have happened if she had hit the hard earth.

The three of us rushed over. Connie lay in the socks, mo-
tionless, with her eyes closed. I thought for sure she was
dead.

"Oh, my gosh!" I shouted, gasping, waving my arms in
the air, my heart pounding.

Sabrina knelt down and felt Connie's pulse. "Connie?
Connie, can you hear me?" she called frantically.

I began clapping my hands in front of Connie's face.

"What are you doing, Daisy?" asked Megan.

"I'm trying to make her come to," I said. "Sometimes a loud noise can do it. I saw it in a movie."

Megan got to her feet. "I'm calling 911."

"Wait!" said Sabrina.

Connie had opened her eyes.

"See? It worked!" I said to Megan.

"Hey, you okay?" Sabrina asked Connie.

"I—I think so," replied Connie. She tried to get up.

"Relax, will you!" said Megan. "For goodness' sake, Connie, you just fell out of a tree!"

"I'm okay," said Connie. "Really."

"Can you move your arms and legs?" asked Sabrina.

Connie moved each of her arms and legs. Nothing seemed to be broken. "Everything seems okay."

"Who's the president of the United States?" I asked.

"What's *that* got to do with anything?" said Megan.

"You're supposed to ask things like that when someone's had a head injury. To make sure their brain is still working okay."

Connie told me who the president was.

"She's okay," I said.

"How'd you fall?" asked Sabrina.

Connie looked startled. "You didn't see her?"

"See who?" I asked.

"Eliza!"

"What are you talking about?" asked Megan.

"She was up in the tree with me!"

"Get out of here!" Megan scoffed.

"I swear!" insisted Connie.

"We didn't see her," said Sabrina.

"Cool! You saw Eliza! That is so awesome!" I lifted my gaze upward. I saw lots of branches and millions of green leaves. If Eliza Baker was perched on a branch, she wasn't revealing herself.

"She didn't make you fall, did she?" asked Sabrina.

Connie shook her head. "No—it's just that she startled me and I lost my grip."

"Lucky you landed on this pile of socks," I said.

"That is lucky," said Connie. "But that's not what saved me. Eliza did."

"Excuse me?" said Megan.

"When I started to fall, I felt Eliza grab me. She held me. She slowed down my fall."

Megan tossed her arms up into the air. "Now I've heard everything!"

I patted Connie on the shoulder. "Hey, nice job getting the socks down."

Connie stared at me. "What are you talking about, Daisy?"

"You got the socks down."

"No, I didn't."

"Sure you did," I said. "See." I pointed to the string of socks that lay on the grass beside Connie.

"I didn't do that," said Connie.

"Of course you did. You just don't remember because of your fall. How else could they have gotten down?"

But then I realized how they got down. Eliza.

30 Sabrina

I KNOW this sounds crazy, but, in a way, I think Connie was secretly kind of glad that she fell out of the tree. We all treated her like a big hero. Plus, she got to *see* Eliza Baker.

Poor Megan, though! After that evening, Daisy gave Megan such a hard time because she was the only one of us whom Eliza Baker hadn't spoken to.

"Like I really care," said Megan one afternoon a few days later as we were eating our lunch. We were sitting on the village green, in the shade of the balm of Gilead. For the first time in weeks, it wasn't steamy hot. It had poured the night before. All the socks in our sock chain were sopping wet. But now it was a beautiful day with lots of blue sky and white puffy clouds. According to the weather report that morning, it was going to be nice for the next few days. There was just one thing forecasters kept mentioning: a big low-pressure system out in the Atlantic Ocean, down by Florida.

"You're just pretending you don't care," said Daisy.

"I'm not pretending, Daisy," replied Megan. She took a swig from her water bottle. "I really don't care."

"Why can't you just admit it bothers you?" asked Daisy before she popped a potato chip in her mouth.

"Because it doesn't," said Megan.

"Not even a little bit?" asked Connie.

"Nope." Megan shook her head.

"Boy, it would sure bother me if I was the only one who hadn't heard her," said Daisy.

"Well, it *doesn't* bother *me*," said Megan. "Maybe if I believed in ghosts, it would bother me, but I don't."

There was something bothering *me*—but I couldn't tell Connie, Megan, or Daisy about it. I didn't dare. The day before, I had made a startling discovery. It happened while I was up in my bedroom, about to go to the bank to make a sockathon deposit. I was flipping through the savings account passbook, looking for a deposit slip, when I spotted something else in the passbook that I had not noticed before. In addition to listing all the deposits that I had made in the last few weeks, the passbook listed something else, all by itself, in its own separate column.

A withdrawal for seventy-five dollars.

It didn't say what the withdrawal was for. Just that a withdrawal had been made on August 14. I was horrified. I don't know why it had never occurred to me that it would be listed. I knew why I hadn't noticed it—I had been deliberately not looking at the deposits each week. I wanted to be surprised at the end of the summer by how much money we had earned. Now I was surprised, all right—surprised and upset. I felt so guilty that I had spent seventy-five dollars of our sockathon money. I still had not told my friends what I had done.

I didn't know how.

"What about you, Sabrina?" I heard Daisy ask.

"What about me?"

"Would it bother you if you were the only one Eliza hadn't contacted?"

"Uh, yeah, I guess so," I said.

"After all that's happened, Megan, how can you not believe in ghosts?" asked Connie.

"Because I don't," Megan replied. She pointed to the Congregational church cemetery that was across the street. "See that grave over there?" she said.

"Which one?" I asked, glancing over.

"That little grave by the side of the church. The one with the red roses on it."

"What about it?" asked Daisy.

"Well, I don't know if you guys have noticed, but every few days someone places new flowers on that grave."

"So?" said Daisy.

"Yeah, so?" I repeated.

"Well," said Megan, "if ghosts really existed, why would a ghost let a person leave flowers every few days? I mean, think about it. What can a ghost do with a bunch of flowers? Nothing. If I were a ghost, I'd tell the person to leave food or something like that. Something that could come in handy if you were dead."

"How do you know the person doesn't leave food?" asked Daisy.

"Because I've never seen any food left on the grave. And besides, people don't leave *food* on graves."

"Maybe the person *does* leave food but the ghost takes it!" Daisy said. "Did you ever think of that? That's why you never see any food!"

"Why, of course, Daisy, that must be it! Why didn't I think of that myself?" said Megan, rolling her eyes.

31 Megan

I COULD have killed Daisy. She was driving me nuts. She kept bugging me about how I was the only one Eliza Baker hadn't spoken to. "Doesn't it bother you?" she kept asking me.

Well, you know what? It did bother me. It bothered me plenty. Not that I would ever admit it. But Daisy had a point.

Sabrina and Daisy claimed they had heard Eliza Baker. Connie claimed she had heard *and* seen her! Why hadn't Eliza Baker shown herself to me? Hey, maybe if she did show herself, it might get me to believe she really existed.

I decided to do something about it. It was the last week in August. I got up super-early one morning—we're talking 7:00 a.m.—and rode my bike to the village green. It was very windy. There were only a few cars and garbage trucks driving around at that hour. I saw a man jogging along Elm Street, but that was all.

It was a perfect time to have a little heart-to-heart chat with Eliza Baker.

"Hey, there," I said as I stood before the huge balm of Gilead tree. I didn't know how else to address a ghost. It's not like I had done it before. "I just came by to see if you wanted to talk."

I waited. There was no response.

"Look," I said, "I know you may have heard me say some not-very-nice things about you. But, hey, it was just talk. I didn't mean anything by them. Really."

I heard something rustle in the tree and peered up. A squirrel was hopping from branch to branch.

"Want me to tell you a little about myself?" I said.

Eliza didn't answer, so I continued.

"Okay, my name is Megan Geherty. I was born in Texas. I'm an only child. My parents got divorced when I was three. My dad lives out in California. I hardly ever see him. My favorite color is blue, my favorite number is seven, I'm a pretty decent soccer player, and someday I'm going to be a fashion designer." I paused and said, "Are you interested in any of this?"

"Very," a voice behind me replied.

I whirled about. Denver was standing just a few feet away, smiling. He was in jeans, a T-shirt, and he had on a Mets cap. He was holding a big roll of masking tape.

"Sorry, I didn't mean to startle you," he apologized.

"You didn't startle me," I blurted out. I couldn't believe he had seen me talking to a tree. How embarrassing!

"Communing with nature, eh?"

"Uh, yeah," I replied. "That's what I was doing."

Denver nodded approvingly. "I saw you when I came out of the church just now. I thought I'd come over and say good morning."

I pointed to the roll of masking tape in his hand. "What's with the tape?" I asked. The moment I said it I realized how nosy I must have sounded. Not to mention disrespectful. After all, he was a minister. I was so embarrassed at having been caught talking to a tree, I wasn't really thinking. Denver didn't seem to mind, though.

"I'm taping the stained-glass windows before Hannah arrives."

"Hannah?"

"The hurricane," said Denver. "They've named it Hannah. Hurricane Hannah. The storm is moving up the coast. It's already hit North Carolina. It's supposed to hit our area by this afternoon."

I glanced up at the sky, which was gray and dark, and then back at Denver.

"Want some help?" I asked. I wanted to get away from the balm of Gilead—and the subject of why I was talking to a tree.

"I'd love some help. Thanks for asking."

Denver walked beside me as I wheeled my bike across the street to the church. He had set up an aluminum stepladder under one of the church's large stained-glass windows. He handed me the roll of masking tape, then climbed up the ladder. I ripped off a long piece and handed it to him.

"You know," said Denver, placing the strip of tape diagonally across the glass, "I ran into your mother the other day."

"You did?" I said. I was surprised that he even knew my mother. Then I remembered that they had met at Boom-boom Brogan's live radio broadcast.

"She was at the nursing home."

"She was probably seeing my Great-aunt Carrie," I said. "What were you doing there?"

"Visiting the seniors," replied Denver. "I go every week. We had a nice long chat, your mother and I."

"You did?" I tore off another long strip of tape.

"We talked about your Great-aunt Carrie," Denver said as he took the tape from me.

"Oh?"

"Your mom told me you never visit her anymore."

"I hate nursing homes."

"Hey, you and me both," said Denver.

I was surprised. "You don't like nursing homes?"

"Can't stand them." He placed the second piece of tape on the glass so that it crossed the first piece. Together, the two strips formed a big **X**.

"But you're a minister," I said. "You *have* to like old people."

"Oh, I didn't say I didn't like the old people *in* the nursing homes. I said I can't stand nursing homes. Your mother told me about what happened to you the last time you visited your great-great-aunt. It sounded horrible."

"It was."

"It's a shame what happens to people when they get old and frail and their minds start to go," said Denver. "They become so scared and lonely. You know what really gets me?"

"What?"

"All those old people were once little babies. Babies who were cuddled and adored. Now nobody wants to get anywhere near them."

"Can we talk about something else?" I asked.

"Sure," said Denver, hopping off the stepladder. I followed him as he carried the ladder around to the cemetery side of the church. He set it up under another stained-glass window. "What do you want to talk about?"

I pointed to the cemetery. "That grave over there," I said. "The one with the flowers."

Denver turned to take a look. "What about it?"

"Every few days someone puts new flowers on that grave," I said. "Do you know anything about it?"

"Well, I don't know who's leaving the flowers," said Denver, "but I can tell you who's buried there. A man named David Meade. He was our church organist."

"Oh! Well, that makes sense."

"How so?"

"His gravestone says 'gatherer of friends.' I couldn't figure out what that meant. Now I do—he must've gathered people together with his music. What did he die of?"

"AIDS," replied Denver.

"Someone sure must miss him to leave flowers week after week."

"David was a very kind man," said Denver as he started up the stepladder again. "He had many friends. People miss him. In a way, his kindness in life has brought him immortality in death."

"Want to hear something really weird?" I asked.

"Absolutely."

"I know you're supposed to be spooked out by cemeteries, but I'm not. In fact, I find I kind of like being around this cemetery. It's so peaceful."

"I agree," said Denver. "You know what I like about cemeteries? Seeing all the dashes."

I frowned. "The *dashes?*"

Denver pointed to an old brown gravestone that was near the edge of the cemetery. The top of the stone was decorated with an angel's head and wings. It was the grave of someone named Jedediah Peck.

"The dash between the dates a person was born and when he died."

"Why do you like seeing *those?*" I asked.

"They're so hopeful."

"They *are?*"

"Think about it," said Denver. "We all get a dash on our gravestone. It doesn't matter if you're rich or poor, young or old, black or white, or from China or the Middle East or even from Timbuktu: we all get one. Everyone is born. Everyone dies. We can't control that. But we *can* control what we do with the dash that's between the day we are born and the day we die. We can change our lives. That's what I find so hopeful. We can change what we do with the dash in between right up until the day we die. It's something I learned from Dr. Martin Luther King, Jr."

"You knew Martin Luther King?" I asked.

"No, but I once heard a sermon by a minister who did know him. That's how I heard about the dashes."

I gave Denver another strip of tape. I watched as he

placed it across the glass. Then I turned and peered at the dash on Jedediah Peck's gravestone.

May 12, 1802—June 30, 1887.

What did he do with his dash? I wondered. It seemed unfair that some people had lots of years within their dashes while others had hardly any years.

Like Eliza.

I began thinking about the dash that would one day be on my gravestone. I hoped there would be a lot of years within my dash. I also hoped I wouldn't get any old dash. I wanted a dash that was different—a dash that was special.

But how do you make a dash special? I was about to ask Denver, but I had a feeling he was probably going to say it was something you had to figure out on your own. Besides, I was pretty sure it wasn't any one thing, but a lot of things. Then suddenly I thought of one thing I could do.

I placed the roll of masking tape on the stepladder beside Denver's feet. "Sorry, Denver," I said, "but I've got to go."

"Where are you going in such a hurry?" he asked. But by then, I was already around the corner of the church and heading for my bike.

MEGAN · 139

32 Connie

THE big storm hit New Elder on August 28—the same day my streak ended. For forty-three straight days, I had delivered my newspapers without once seeing Mrs. Campbell. It was a great streak. I didn't want to see it end.

It was about nine o'clock in the morning, and I was rushing to deliver my newspapers before the storm hit. It wasn't supposed to arrive until later that afternoon, but all the TV and radio stations were making such a big deal out of it, they made it sound like it was going to arrive any second. The storm had started out as a hurricane, but it had been downgraded to a tropical storm. Still, the weather people were warning everyone about its heavy rains and gale-force winds. The front page of that day's *New Elder Times* had a big photograph of two men who owned a convenience store near a beach in New Jersey. They were boarding up a store window with plywood sheets.

When I got to Mrs. Campbell's house, I tossed her newspaper onto her front porch. I was hurrying off when I heard a voice call out: "Wait just a minute!"

I stopped. Groaned. Swung around. Mrs. Campbell had come out of her house. My streak was over.

"Do you know anything about this?" she asked. She held up a sheet of paper.

I nearly died. It was the sockathon flyer that Daisy had put in her newspaper.

"It's a flyer," I replied innocently.

"I know it's a flyer," said Mrs. Campbell. "Do you know how it got in my newspaper?"

She stared at me with such intensity, I had to glance away. "We put it in," I confessed.

"We?"

"My friend Daisy and I."

"*You're* one of the girls who are raising money to buy a brace for the balm of Gilead tree?"

I nodded. "Yes."

"You know that tree is rotting, don't you?" she said.

"Yes, we know."

"It's going to keep right on rotting, even with a brace. You girls are just wasting your time."

"We are not wasting our time!" I exclaimed.

Mrs. Campbell looked surprised. I guess she never thought *I'd* talk back to her. I never thought I'd talk back to her, either. But I had had enough of Mrs. Campbell and her dumb old opinions on everything.

"I beg your pardon?" she said.

"We're *not* wasting our time," I said. "That tree is over two hundred and seventy-five years old! George Washington slept under it! It's part of this country's history! We should be doing everything possible to save it!"

Then I added quickly, "Well, I've got to go. Good-bye."

"You know that tree has a bad history," said Mrs. Campbell as I started down the porch steps.

I stopped and looked back at her. "Oh, you mean about Eliza Baker?"

Mrs. Campbell stared at me. She appeared startled. "Oh, so you know about that silly old ghost story?"

"It's not a silly old ghost story! I've *seen* her!" I blurted out. As soon as I said it, I realized my mistake. I had broken the pinkie promise that I'd made with Sabrina, Megan, and Daisy.

"You've *seen* her?" said Mrs. Campbell, looking at me intently. "What do you mean you've seen her?"

"I've seen her," I repeated. "Up in the tree." Then I told Mrs. Campbell about the incident in the tree. I couldn't help it: once I got started talking about it, I couldn't stop. The one thing I didn't tell Mrs. Campbell was what Eliza had looked like. It made me sad to think of Eliza looking all bruised up.

After I told Mrs. Campbell about Eliza, she just scoffed. "Rubbish!" she said. "There's no such thing as ghosts!"

"I don't care whether you believe me or not. Eliza Baker was right there beside me on the branch. I could've touched her, she was that close. She even spoke to me."

"She spoke to you?" said Mrs. Campbell. "And what, may I ask, did she say?"

"She told me, 'Don't be such an old lady.'"

Mrs. Campbell sort of flinched. I guess she wasn't expecting a ghost to say something like that. She was silent for a while, so I said, "Well, I better get going. My friends are waiting for me at the tree."

"I'll drive you there," said Mrs. Campbell.

Now it was my turn to be startled. I thought I was hearing things. "Uh, that's okay."

"I have to drive into town, anyway. I need to buy flashlight batteries at the store. I want to be prepared in case the electricity goes out during the storm. I can drop you off at the village green."

"Thanks," I said, "but I still have more newspapers to deliver."

"How many more?"

"Well, just a couple."

"I'll drive you to their houses," said Mrs. Campbell. "Then I'll drive you to the village green. It's right on the way to the supermarket. It's no trouble at all for me to drop you off."

I was about to say no again, but then I thought of something. I thought of how shocked Sabrina, Megan, and Daisy would be to see me hop out of Mrs. Campbell's car.

I couldn't resist.

"Well . . . if it's not too much trouble," I said, smiling. "Okay."

33 Daisy

SABRINA and I were on the village green, doing everything we could possibly think of to protect our sock chain and the pile of socks before the storm hit. We couldn't protect the entire sock chain, of course—it was almost three miles long—but we thought we should try to protect those socks that were on the village green.

First, we secured the sock chain to the ground with wire wickets that Sabrina had taken from her parents' croquet set. Then we unfolded a big, blue plastic tarpaulin that I'd gotten from my garage. We placed the tarp over the sock pile.

I held the tarp down while Sabrina stuck metal stakes into each small hole along the edges of the tarp. While Sabrina was pounding a stake into the grass with a wooden croquet mallet, I spotted two figures walking toward us across the village green from Elm Street. One was a tall, skinny, white-haired lady with a cane. She was wearing a beige raincoat and a floppy rain hat. The other figure was a girl in shorts and a T-shirt.

I thought I was going to faint. *I must be seeing things,* I told myself.

34 Sabrina

Tell me I'm seeing things!" said Daisy.

I didn't know what Daisy was talking about. I was on my knees, with a wooden croquet mallet in my hands. I was pounding a tent stake into the ground so we could tie down the tarpaulin.

"What are you talking about?" I asked.

Daisy pointed in the direction of Elm Street, just behind me. I swung around. I nearly had a heart attack. Mrs. Campbell, cane in hand, was limping toward us—with Connie at her side.

"Oh, my gosh!" I cried, scrambling to my feet. "What's Mrs. Campbell doing here?"

Mrs. Campbell stopped before the balm of Gilead tree. She leaned against her cane and gazed at the tree as if it was a huge monument or something.

Connie came over to Daisy and me. "Hey, guys," she said, as casual as could be.

"What's going on?" I whispered.

Connie grinned. Evidently, she thought it was amusing

that we were so startled to see Mrs. Campbell. Like she wouldn't have been, too.

"Mrs. Campbell drove me here," said Connie. "She wanted to see our sock chain."

I was about to ask Connie more questions when I heard a loud "Ugh!" from Mrs. Campbell.

"Will you look at how long this grass is!" Mrs. Campbell cried, a disgusted look on her face, as she waved her cane at the grass—which really didn't look all that long to me. "You'd think someone had never heard of a lawn mower! When I came here in June, I was appalled at how shabby everything looked. I came after I heard on the radio that the balm of Gilead was to be cut down. I hadn't set foot on the village green in years. I was curious to see the tree one last time before it was cut down. My heavens! You should've seen the way the village green looked that day! What a mess! Litter was everywhere! I got right back in my car and went straight home and wrote a letter to the editor and dropped it off at the newspaper. The next day the story of the balm of Gilead was front-page news in *The New Elder Times*. But of course my letter to the editor was nowhere to be found in the paper.

"I wish you girls could have seen the village green the way it used to be. This was years ago, before any of you were born. Back then, families would gather on summer evenings and on Sunday afternoons and listen to brass bands in the gazebo. The parents would spend time together and chat while the children caught fireflies or played games like hide-and-seek and red rover. Oh, those were the days! Now families just sit at home and stare at their TV sets! When I was here in June, I saw a man talking on his cell phone. Instead of enjoying the moment, he was yakking away on his phone! Can you believe it? Honestly! It's a shame what's become of our civilization! It really is! Our civilization has become as rotten as . . . as this balm of Gilead tree!" Mrs. Campbell lifted the end of her cane and pointed it at the huge old tree.

The strangest thing happened then. The tree began to quiver. Then shake.

At first, I thought it was just the wind blowing the branches around. But it wasn't the wind. No way! The tree was shaking too violently.

Terrified, I dashed over to the gazebo. Daisy and Connie were right behind me. They looked terrified, too. Mrs. Campbell was still standing by the tree. She seemed frozen by fear. She let out a shriek.

"My Godfrey!" she exclaimed, her voice trembling. "Stop it this minute, do you hear me? Stop it!"

The tree stopped shaking. Just like that.

Mrs. Campbell looked really shaken up. She turned to go back to her car. As she moved off, a small branch of the balm of Gilead tree caught her hat and pulled it off her head.

"My hat!" she cried, reaching for her head.

"I'll get it," I said, and I hurried down the gazebo steps. The branch was only a foot or so above my head—within easy reach. But when I leaped up to grab it, the branch bounced upward.

I tried again. The same thing happened. Then it happened again.

"Let me try," said Daisy.

The same thing happened to Daisy. And to Connie, too, when she tried.

I stepped back so I could make a running leap. Suddenly, I felt a drop of rain on my head. Then another, and another. Then it began to pour.

I ran toward the tree and took a huge leap. Just as my fingers were about to touch the brim of the hat, the branch swung upward.

I was so frustrated I stamped my foot on the ground.

"Oh, dear!" I heard Mrs. Campbell say.

Then, to my amazement, I thought I heard Mrs. Campbell chuckle. I was sure I had just imagined it, though.

I tried again to grab the hat. Again, I missed. "Grrrrrrrr!" I cried, clenching my fists.

This time there was no mistake about it. Mrs. Campbell let out a loud chuckle.

"Now, now!" she said as she stood in the rain, laughing. "Let's not lose our tempers."

Connie, Daisy, and I glanced at one another. We all had the same okay-this-is-really-weird expressions on our faces. I guess the three of us must have looked pretty silly, the way we kept jumping up over and over again. It was strange to hear Mrs. Campbell laugh. I was surprised she even knew how.

As Daisy went to take another leap, a strong gust of wind came up. It blew the hat off the branch and onto the lawn. The hat danced across the grass and became entangled in some bushes by the gazebo. I dashed over and grabbed it.

"Hooray!" shouted Mrs. Campbell, clapping.

I handed Mrs. Campbell her hat. She thanked me and then stuck it back on her head—crookedly. She chuckled and said, "Look at us! We're all drenched! The storm must be here. We'd better go."

Connie, Daisy, and I helped Mrs. Campbell to her car. She needed help, too—the wind had become even more gusty. If we hadn't been there to steady her, she probably would have blown away like her hat.

Mrs. Campbell was about to climb into her car when she stopped and reached into her straw handbag.

"This is for your sockathon," she said, holding out a fifty-dollar bill.

We all stared at her.

Mrs. Campbell laughed at us. "You should see your faces," she said, placing the bill in my wet palm. "Go on, put the money in your pocket so you don't lose it."

I did what she said. Then Mrs. Campbell got into her car and started up the motor.

"Tell me that wasn't weird," I said as we watched her drive off down Elm Street.

"That *was* weird!" said Connie.

"Totally weird!" said Daisy.

"I can't believe she gave us fifty dollars!" I said.

"I can't believe what happened at the tree!" said Daisy. "The way Old Balmy was shaking? That freaked me out!"

"It freaked me out, too!" said Connie.

"Too bad Megan missed it all," I said.

"She misses everything!" said Daisy.

"Where is Megan?" I asked, peering at Connie.

Connie shrugged. "I thought she was with you guys."

"We thought she was with you," said Daisy.

I glanced around. The telephone wires on Elm Street were swaying back and forth in the wet, gusty wind.

"Where on earth could she be?" I said.

35 Megan

IT's funny how a little thing can make such a big impression on you. But that's what happened when Denver told me about the dashes on the gravestones. It just made a lot of sense to me. I don't know why, but it did.

After I left Denver, I hopped on my bike and began peddling. I knew exactly where to go: the Chatham Green Nursing Home.

It takes about a half hour to get to the nursing home from the center of New Elder. But that's by car. By bike, it took me close to an hour and twenty minutes. By the time I pulled into the nursing-home parking lot, it was nearly 10:30 and my legs were aching.

It felt weird walking into the nursing home without Mom. As I headed down the main hallway, I kept expecting a nurse to pop out from one of the rooms and tell me that no kids were allowed in the nursing home without a parent or guardian. But that didn't happen. I also kept an eye out for that old guy with Alzheimer's. I didn't see him, though. I was glad about that. Well, sort of glad. To be honest, I felt kind of guilty about the way I had acted. Maybe Mom was right—maybe I had overreacted. I mean, he was just an old guy. If I saw him again, I was going to try and be a little nicer. But I didn't see him.

When I got to Great-aunt Carrie's room, I stood in her doorway for a minute. The lamp beside her bed was off and her window blinds were lowered, making the room very dark. I had to wait for my eyes to adjust to the light. Slowly, the big smudge that was in the middle of the room material-ized into a bed. A small frail body lay curled on the bed, half-covered by a pink blanket.

I went over to the bed and turned on the lamp. "Hi, Great-aunt Carrie," I said.

For a moment, I thought Great-aunt Carrie was asleep. But then her eyes opened and she peered up at me. I had never been this close to Great-aunt Carrie. She had brown eyes that were hazy with age. She stared at me with this questioning look in her eyes.

I smiled and said, "Hey, Great-aunt Carrie, it's me—Megan."

Great-aunt Carrie said nothing. She just stared.

Gathering up my courage, I reached over and picked up her hand. I could feel her bones, her hand was so old, so fragile. It really creeped me out.

This better earn me a good dash, I thought.

"How are you?" I asked. "I—uh—just thought I'd drop by and—um—see how you were doing."

I didn't know what else to say.

"I don't know if Mom's told you," I went on, "but I've

been busy this summer raising money to buy a brace for the old balm of Gilead tree that's on the village green."

This is like talking to a tree, I thought.

"You know the tree I'm talking about, don't you? The balm of Gilead that's on the village green? Well, it's rotting. The town was going to cut it down, but we—my friends and I—decided to raise money and try and save it by buying a brace. You'll never guess how we're raising the money. We're making a sock chain. It's kind of a wacky idea, I admit, but people are donating socks and money."

I explained how the sockathon worked, and how we'd been on the radio. I knew I was just babbling, but the thought of sitting with Great-aunt Carrie in silence scared me.

"We've raised a lot of money," I said. "Over a thousand dollars. Pretty cool, huh?"

Great-aunt Carrie's eyes had closed. Was she asleep? I couldn't tell. "Well, Great-aunt Carrie, I just came by to say hi."

I came all this way just to say hi. What am I, nuts?

I started to pull my hand out of hers. Suddenly Great-aunt Carrie opened her eyes. She held onto my hand with an iron-tight grip. It really spooked me.

Now stay calm, I told myself.

"I have to go, Great-aunt Carrie," I said. I made another attempt to pull my hand away, but she would not let go.

Then, all of sudden, Great-aunt Carrie tugged at my hand, pulling me down close beside her.

"Thank you, Megan," she whispered in a weak, feeble voice I could barely hear.

I was shocked. For a moment, all I could do was stare at Great-aunt Carrie's ancient, wrinkled face.

Great-aunt Carrie spoke to me! She never talks! Not even to Mom! But she spoke to me! And she knows my name! She knows I'm Megan!

I felt my eyes growing wet with tears. I blinked, and a tear slid down my face.

I leaned down and gave Great-aunt Carrie a kiss on the cheek. I was startled. I thought for sure that kissing her would be like kissing a lizard.

But I was wrong. Her cheek was as soft as a baby's.

36 Connie

SABRINA, Daisy, and I were all freaking out. We had no idea where Megan was. We tried to call her on her cell phone, but she didn't pick up. Then we tried calling her house. But all we got was the answering machine.

So we split up to search for her. Sabrina and Daisy got on their bikes to ride around town. Since I didn't have my bike, I looked in the Congregational church. Megan wasn't there. I didn't see Denver, either.

I stepped outside. It was dark and raining furiously. I raced down the church steps and across Elm Street and onto the wet mushy grass of the village green. I ran up to the gazebo. That was where Sabrina, Daisy, and I had agreed to meet. I was the first one back. I stood in the gazebo, glancing around the village green, hoping to see them. I could hear the rain pounding on the gazebo roof. Water gushed off the eaves. The branches of the balm of Gilead were tossing about in the fierce wind. I felt so sorry for Eliza. She had no place to go during the storm. But then I thought that Eliza had probably been in hundreds of storms. This was nothing to her. Still, it would be nice if she didn't have to spend the rest of eternity stuck in storms or have bruises all over her body or to even have to be a ghost, for that matter.

Then I thought about Mrs. Campbell and all the freaky things that had happened when she came to the village green. It all seemed so strange.

Daisy was the first to return, then Sabrina. Neither one had seen Megan.

"What should we do?" I asked.

"I don't know," said Sabrina. She ran her fingers through her wet hair. She looked like she'd fallen into a swimming pool with all her clothes on. We all looked that way.

"Maybe she's with her mother," I suggested.

"Look!" cried Daisy, pointing toward Church Street.

Through the slanted sheets of rain, I saw a person hunched over on a bike, peddling in our direction. It was Megan. She looked absolutely soaked. She rode her bike across Elm Street, then pedaled through a huge pool of water that had formed on the village green. She threw down her bike and raced up the gazebo steps.

"Is it raining or what?" she cried.

"Where have you been?" asked Sabrina.

"We've been trying to call you on your cell phone!" said Daisy.

Megan wiped the rain from her face. "I guess I forgot to turn it on."

"We thought something terrible had happened to you," I said.

"Sorry, guys, I didn't mean to scare you," said Megan. "I was visiting my Great-aunt Carrie."

"You were *what?*" said Daisy.

"Well, you know I hadn't seen her most of the summer," said Megan, as if this explained everything.

I glanced over at the balm of Gilead tree. It was really swaying in the wind. I knew our parents were probably worried about us. "Hey, guys, we better get home," I said.

Nobody argued. We said good-bye. Megan and Daisy headed off in the direction of their homes while Sabrina and I went off toward ours.

I ran the whole way. Sabrina rode her bike beside me. She had trouble keeping it steady in the wind and driving rain. As I dashed down street after street, dodging puddles, I kept glancing up at the power lines. They were heaving up and down in the wind. I just prayed they wouldn't snap and drop down on us.

"See ya!" I shouted when we finally got to my house.

As I started up my driveway, Sabrina yelled, "Think the sock chain will hold?"

"I sure hope so!" I yelled back. Then, turning, I ran into my dry garage.

37 Daisy

WHILE the storm raged outside my bedroom window, I sat at my desk, trying to think of how we could raise more money to buy a brace for Old Balmy. I was doodling on a yellow pad of paper, racking my brain, when I heard a wet *smack!* at my window.

Startled, I sprang out of my chair. Something small and dark was clinging to the rain-smeared glass. *A strong gust of wind must have banged a poor bird into it,* I thought.

But then I heard another smack over at my other window. A small, dark object had hit this window, too!

I went to take a closer look. I was shocked. It wasn't a bird at all—it was . . . a sock!

A sopping-wet man's dark argyle sock!

I peered out my window. The oak tree on my front lawn was swaying in the wind, and the rain was pelting down on everything. Our front lawn looked like a swamp. I strained my eyes to see what was happening to the sock chain that ran in front of our house.

It was gone!

The last time I had looked—less than five minutes ago—

the sock chain had been flopping wildly about in the wind. But since then, the storm had ripped it apart. Socks were blowing and swirling about all over the place—across my front yard and driveway, down the street, in the neighbors' front yards.

I gasped. *Omigod! It's like a washing machine out there!*

38 Sabrina

THAT afternoon of the storm, I sat on my bed and tried to read one of the books on my mother's list. But I couldn't concentrate. I kept thinking about the seventy-five dollars of the sockathon money that I had given away. What would my friends say when they found out? They were sure to find out. Daisy knew how much money we had raised, right down to the very last penny.

If only I had seventy-five dollars of my own, I thought, *I could make up the difference and none of them would ever know.*

But I didn't have seventy-five dollars. I had maybe fifteen dollars saved up, if that. I could just hear my mother: "Well, Sabrina, if you did your chores like I asked you to, you'd have allowance money."

I came downstairs. Daddy was in the family room, in front of the TV. He was watching the Weather Channel. He was following the progress of the storm.

"Hi, Daddy," I said. "Can I do anything for you?"

"Sure, you can sit down and keep me company."

"No, I mean do you have any chores I can do?" I said. "You know, so I can make money."

"Oh, you mean for your sockathon?" asked Daddy. "I can't think of anything. Maybe your mom has something for you."

"Where is she?"

"Down in the cellar," he said. "She's scraping porch furniture. You know how she is."

I did know. My mother always had to keep busy. Even during a fierce storm.

"Want some help?" I asked as I came down the cellar stairs.

My mother was over by the washing machine and dryer. She was kneeling beside a blue metal porch chair. She was in her work clothes—ratty sneakers, old jeans, a torn T-shirt, and cloth work gloves. She was using a wire brush to scrape off the chair's blue paint.

My mother looked up at me and said, "I'm okay, thanks."

"Want me to scrape for you?" I asked. "I'll do it for five dollars."

"Sabrina, you've been working hard all summer raising money for your sockathon," said my mother. "I think you should take the afternoon off and relax."

"I don't want to relax," I replied. "I want to earn money. C'mon, what do you say? Want me to scrape?"

"No, I want you to relax," said my mother. "You can read one of the books on your list."

"There must be *something* I can do for you!"

My mother set the wire brush down on the bench and stood up. She pulled off her work gloves, blew a wisp of black hair that had fallen across her forehead, and came over to me.

"I've been meaning to talk with you," she said.

"You have? About what?"

"About you."

"*Me?*"

My mother nodded.

I suddenly had this terrible sinking feeling that my mother knew about the seventy-five-dollar withdrawal I had made.

"You've done something I didn't think you would ever do," she said.

"I have?"

"I thought you'd give up your sockathon after a few days," said my mother. "I thought as soon as you found out how difficult it is to raise money, you'd quit. But you didn't. You stuck with it. I'm very proud of you."

That's because you don't know about the cashier's check. You don't know I spent other people's money.

My mother placed her arm around my shoulders and gave me a little kiss on the side of my head.

But I needed more than just a kiss.

"Can I have a hug?" I asked.

My mother didn't ask why. She put both arms around me and gave me a big, comforting hug. I hadn't let her do that to me since I was around six years old.

It was just what I needed. It made me feel all warm and cozy inside—the way I used to feel when I was a little

kid and I'd rush inside the house after something had upset me.

I knew I was home, where I was loved. Where, even if I
did something wrong, I'd still be loved.

I told Mom about the seventy-five-dollar withdrawal
then. I thought she'd be very disappointed in me, but she
wasn't. In fact, she hugged me even tighter.

39 Megan

DURING the storm, Mom and I sat in our TV room and watched *The Wizard of Oz*. We have the movie on DVD. It's one of our favorites. But my mind wasn't really on *The Wizard of Oz*. It was on Great-aunt Carrie. I was still thinking about how she had spoken to me.

And that she knew who I was!

I still had not told Mom about my visit to the nursing home. I was dying to. But Mom had been in a bad mood when I got home and yelled at me.

"Look at you!" she cried. "You're sopping wet! Where have you been all this time? Do you know how worried I was! I've been calling and calling your cell phone! You're supposed to have it on!"

I figured I'd wait until Mom was in a better mood before I told her about Great-aunt Carrie. The thing was, I felt very special that Great-aunt Carrie had spoken to me. I didn't want Mom to ruin the feeling. Which is what would have happened if I'd told her about it when she was in a bad mood.

We were near the end of the movie. We were right at the

part where Dorothy was clicking her heels together to go back home when, suddenly, the electricity gave out. The TV screen went black, and all the lights in the room went off. The storm had knocked out the power.

Mom and I moved to the kitchen. Mom lit some candles that she kept in a drawer and set them on the table. She seemed to be in a better mood now. So I decided I'd tell her about my visit with Great-aunt Carrie. I was all set to say something when the phone rang. Mom and I looked at each other in surprise.

"The phone works?" I said. I figured it went out when the electricity did. I sprang out of my chair and picked up the phone by the refrigerator. "Hello?"

"Hello," said a woman's voice. "Is this the Geherty residence?"

"Yes, it is," I said.

"This is Martha Walker at the Chatham Green Nursing Home. Is Mrs. Geherty at home?"

"Yes, she is. Hold on, please."

"Who is it?" whispered Mom, with a puzzled look, as I handed her the phone.

"Some lady from the Chatham Green Nursing Home."

Mom made a sort of grim face and then said, "Hello?" into the phone.

Mom listened for a moment. "What time did it happen?" she asked. "I see. . . . Well, I'm glad she didn't suffer."

Mom was on the phone for several minutes. Then she thanked the woman for calling and hung up. I stared at her, waiting for her to say something.

Mom let out a deep breath. She had tears in her eyes. "Great-aunt Carrie died in her sleep this afternoon."

"She's dead?"

Mom nodded and wiped her eyes with her hands.

Omigod! I thought. *I bet I'm the last person Great-aunt Carrie spoke to! The last person on Earth!*

It was then that I told Mom about my visit.

40 Connie

AFTER Sabrina and I said good-bye in front of my driveway, I dashed into the house. Mom was furious. "Where have you been?" she demanded. I guess she was really worried about me. She told me to go straight upstairs to my room and get out of my wet clothes.

I put on some dry ones and came downstairs to the family room, where Mom and Dad were watching TV. Dad had the remote. He kept switching from channel to channel to see what was being reported about the storm. We saw the damage it had done in North Carolina. A beach in Virginia, where shingles had been blown off a cottage. Downtown Washington, D.C. A town called Oceanside, New Jersey. New York City, where streets were flooded. Another beach, this one on Long Island.

While I watched TV, I tried to piece together all the things that had happened at the village green. It was so strange the way the balm of Gilead tree had shaken like crazy when Mrs. Campbell showed up. It was as if Eliza Baker couldn't stand Mrs. Campbell. Who could blame her? All that ranting and raving! Just like an old lady. A bitter old lady. Yet Mrs.

Campbell did give us fifty dollars for our sockathon. That didn't seem like something a bitter old lady would do. Then I remembered something else: Mrs. Campbell said she went to the village green in June after she heard the balm of Gilead was going to be cut down. That would have been the same day Sabrina heard Eliza Baker's voice.

"Wow!" I heard Dad say.

He was reacting to what was on TV. The TV showed rescue workers in a rowboat motoring in the pouring rain along a flooded street. They were going from house to house, searching for people who might be trapped in their houses.

I sure hope Mrs. Campbell is watching this, I thought. I wanted her to see that not all of civilization was rotten.

We watched the progress of the storm for the rest of the afternoon. Our part of town never lost power the way Megan's did. Toward the end of the storm, our phone rang. Mom went into the kitchen to answer it. "It's for you, Connie," she said, handing me the phone.

"Hello?" I said.

"Connie, can you meet?" It was Daisy. Her voice sounded very upset. All trembly and urgent.

"Is everything okay, Daisy?"

I heard a sniffle. Then a little sob.

"Daisy?" I said. "Are you okay?"

"No, I'm not okay!" she replied. "We've all got to meet right now!"

"Now?" I gazed out the kitchen window at my backyard. The storm, for the most part, had passed. It was just driz-

zling. The sky had begun to brighten. "What's wrong, Daisy?"

"It's the sock chain!" she said.

"What about it?"

"It's . . . it's been blown to smithereens!"

41 Daisy

WHAT a disaster! I thought as I peddled my bike toward town. I kept wiping tears from my eyes, I was so upset.

Socks were everywhere. In the street. On front lawns. In people's driveways. Socks were clinging to shrubs and clogging up drain sewers. I even saw a sock dangling from a telephone wire.

Our sockathon was over. No doubt about it. It made me mad to think we wouldn't get to end it the way we had planned, with a big street fair.

The gray, overcast sky was quickly breaking apart. A large patch of blue sky was overhead, and the sun was shining brightly. Everything looked so sparkly clean.

When I got to King Street, a huge branch was lying across the pavement. The branch had knocked down a power line. Thick black wires lay across the pavement. So I rode over to Sycamore Street. As I turned onto Hill Street, I spotted Sabrina and Connie on their bikes just up ahead. I peddled like a maniac and caught up with them.

"Can you believe all these socks?" I said as I weaved in and out of the socks that were lying like worms in the wet street.

"We'll be cleaning up socks for weeks," said Connie.

"Try months," said Sabrina.

Turning down Elm Street, Sabrina abruptly jammed on her brakes.

"Hey, Sabrina, what are you doing?" I cried as I swerved to avoid crashing into the rear of her bike. My tires skidded across the wet pavement.

And then I saw why Sabrina had stopped.

The balm of Gilead tree was no longer standing. It had blown over in the storm. The tree lay stretched across the village green, from one end to the other, like a huge dead giant. It had just missed smashing the gazebo. The storm had split the trunk right in half, about ten feet up from the ground. Huge, jagged splinters of yellow wood rose up into the air. A small crowd stood around the tree, gawking. Some kids were climbing on the leafy branches as if the tree was some sort of amusement-park attraction.

"Oh, no!" I gasped.

"This is horrible!" cried Sabrina.

Over on Church Street, Megan appeared on her bike, peddling furiously. She came whizzing up to us and skidded to a stop.

"Poor tree!" she said.

"Poor Eliza!" said Connie. "What do you think has happened to her?"

None of us had a clue.

Two Weeks Later

42 Sabrina

"You'd think *someone* would have one," I said.

"Yeah, you'd think," said Megan.

"Well, it's not like we didn't try," said Connie.

"Yeah, we must've called every tree place in the area," said Daisy. "Nobody has a balm of Gilead tree."

"Well, I guess a dogwood tree isn't such a bad substitute," I sighed. "I mean, it does have nice blossoms in the spring."

The four of us were sitting at my kitchen table. It was a Tuesday afternoon. We had come straight from school to my house. We were back in school again. Megan and I were in the same class—we had Mrs. Rodriguez for sixth grade. Daisy had gotten Ms. Proto, and Connie had Mr. Billeci.

We had all wondered what kids would say to us when we got back to school. Megan was sure they were going to tease us for doing something as wacky as a sockathon over our summer vacation. But no one did. At least, no one said anything to our faces. In fact, a few kids said they thought the sockathon was a really cool idea. But even if kids had teased us, I wouldn't have cared. I mean, hey, we were on the radio.

And we raised over $1,000. How many kids can say that? Not many!

One girl, Lisa Meyers, came up to me in gym class and said she felt so sorry for us because we had spent all that time and effort to raise money for the balm of Gilead tree only to see the tree fall down. She made it sound like we had wasted our whole summer. It's funny, though. I don't feel like we wasted our summer. Not at all.

A lot had happened since the storm had toppled the balm of Gilead tree and ended our sockathon. The very next morning, some men from a tree-removal company arrived in trucks and sawed up the tree. All day long you could hear the whine of chain saws as the men in hard hats carved the tree up into smaller and smaller pieces. The branches were pushed into a wood chipper.

After being a landmark for more than 275 years, the balm of Gilead tree had been cut up and carted off in less than a day. Now just a trace of sawdust was all that remained of the magnificent tree.

The socks had disappeared, too. A big orange street sweeper swept up all the socks lying in the streets and parking lots. People all over town pitched in and helped us pick up the rest of them that were on the village green and lawns and driveways. In a way, it was funny. We had planned to end the sockathon with a big finale. People would come together on the last day and tie all the loose ends of the sock chain so it would be one long continuous string of socks. People had come together, all right—to pick socks up off the ground.

Megan missed everything—as usual. The day after the

storm, she and her mother left town to attend the funeral of Megan's Great-aunt Carrie. The funeral was held in upstate New York, in a small town where she had grown up.

Two weeks after the storm, we still had no idea what had happened to Eliza Baker. For days we bicycled over to the village green, hoping she might somehow let us know that she was okay. Or, better yet, that she was finally at peace and in heaven. If only she'd give us *some* sort of sign. But she didn't. Daisy, Connie, and I all felt bad for Megan. She was the only one of us who Eliza hadn't spoken to. But Megan didn't seem to mind. She said her Great-aunt Carrie had spoken to her—and that was enough for her.

"Well, since we can't find a balm of Gilead tree, I say we get the biggest dogwood tree we can buy," said Megan, glancing around the table at us. "How much money do we have to spend?"

"Well, according to my figures, our sockathon raised one thousand, seven hundred and sixty-one dollars, and thirty-two cents," said Daisy.

I took a deep breath.

"Uh, guys, there's something I have to tell you," I said. "It's about the sockathon money. I—um—I—uh—well, I spent some of it."

"You did *what?*" said Megan, aghast.

"Don't worry—it's all been replaced," I said quickly.

"How much did you spend?"

"Seventy-five dollars. But it's been replaced."

"What did you spend it on?" asked Daisy.

"Well, actually, I didn't really spend it—I gave it away."

"To *who?*" asked Connie.

"To a charity," I replied. "But like I said, I've already put the money back."

"Then why are you telling us this?" asked Megan.

"It's part of the agreement."

"What agreement?" asked Connie.

"The one I made with my mom. She gave me the money. But I had to agree to two things. One was that I had to tell you guys about it."

"What was the other thing?" asked Daisy.

"I have to finish the books on her reading list."

43 Mrs. Campbell

MY Godfrey, was it hot! Hot and steamy! It must have been close to ninety degrees that day the tree-planting ceremony was to take place. Still, a big crowd gathered for the event.

Including me.

Connie had knocked on my door earlier that week when she was delivering my newspaper and told me about the ceremony. She asked if I would like to attend. She said that she and her friends had used the money they had raised from the sockathon and bought a big dogwood tree.

"Good heavens, a *dogwood* tree?" I said, surprised.

"We wanted to buy a balm of Gilead tree, but none of the tree places around here had any," Connie explained. "So we got a dogwood. It was actually the mayor's idea to get a dogwood. It will be a really huge one, planted where the old balm of Gilead was. You know, to replace it."

Not that a 275-year-old tree could ever really be replaced, I thought. Since the storm, I had driven into town several times. It saddened me to drive past the village green. It looked so lonely and empty without that great balm of Gilead tree.

I arrived early for the ceremony. It was going to be a big event—*The New Elder Times* had an article about it on its front page. A local TV camera crew was over there. From what I understand, when the girls went to Nancy Sargent, the mayor, and asked permission to plant the tree, Mrs. Sargent and the other town officials liked the idea so much they decided to turn it into a special event. Workmen erected a platform, set up a podium, and put out rows of folding metal chairs so people could sit. Programs had been printed up and placed on each seat.

Before the ceremony began, Connie introduced me to her parents. I also met Sabrina, Megan, and Daisy's parents, as well as Denver, the minister of the Congregational church, and the mayor. Then I took a seat in the first row, directly in front of the spot where the old balm of Gilead had once stood. There was a large hole where the new tree was to be planted. Connie was right: it was a huge tree. Apparently, a tractor-trailer truck had to deliver it, it was so big. The dogwood now stood in the hole, its roots in a huge ball of earth wrapped in burlap.

At noon, the ceremony began. Connie, Sabrina, Megan, and Daisy took their seats up on the platform. Connie glanced at me and smiled. I gave her a little wave back.

Mrs. Sargent started things off. She stood at the podium and gave the world's dullest speech. She talked about the important role that the balm of Gilead had played in the town's history. She just went on and on.

Oh, come on, I thought. *We're here to plant a tree, not listen to you. Get on with it!*

I closed my eyes and fanned myself with my program.

Ugh, it was hot! It felt just like that day years and years ago when Franklin Roosevelt came to New Elder. It had started out as such a good day. The gazebo was decorated with American flags. A brass band was playing, and there was a parade down Elm Street. And, of course, there was the Democratic candidate for president, Franklin Delano Roosevelt.

Now *there* was someone who could give a speech!

The crowd had been enormous. Those were the days when men and women dressed up and wore hats. It was almost impossible to see the gazebo over all those hatted heads—particularly if you were two eleven-year-old girls.

It was just like Eliza to suggest that we climb the balm of Gilead tree to get a better view.

And it was just like me to go along—and to be scared stiff.

All these years later, I can still see the startled expression on Eliza's face when the branch that she was perched on broke from under her.

And I can still hear the dreadful sound of her scream as she crashed through the branches. To this day, I still think about the *if only*'s.

If only I had been brave and climbed up to the top of the tree, Eliza wouldn't have come down to help me and she might still be alive. . . .

If only I had not stopped at that branch . . .

If only I had grabbed her hand as she started to fall . . .

If only . . .

I was haunted by what had happened. After grade school, I attended New Elder's high school, and then went off to college. After college, I got married. Years later, I returned to New Elder—but not as Ginny Doyle. I returned as Mrs. Virginia Campbell. I was no longer the timid little girl who had followed Eliza Baker up the tree. I had done something Eliza could never do—I had grown up.

I had grown up and become a dull, boring, set-in-her-ways, opinionated adult.

An old lady!

By then, I figured everyone had forgotten about Ginny Doyle. Which was fine by me. I, too, wanted to forget the whole horrible incident. But I couldn't. Over the years, I heard stories about how the balm of Gilead tree was haunted by Eliza. But I considered these nothing more than silly ghost stories that had been made up by children with wild imaginations. Still, I went out of my way to avoid the tree with its unhappy memories. When I did finally visit the village green, back in June, I was overcome with emotion at seeing the tree again. I was also upset by how shabby everything looked. I guess I got a little carried away. I'm sure Eliza must have heard me complaining. But at that point, I didn't believe in Eliza—or, rather, in her ghost.

But that changed the day of the storm.

There is no doubt in my mind why the tree behaved so strangely that day. It was because of Eliza. I know she was in that tree. And I know why she acted the way she did. She was telling me to stop being such an old lady—just the way she used to.

But now that the Balm of Gilead was gone, what had happened to Eliza?

"Thank you!" Mrs. Sargent's voice said over the loudspeaker as she stepped away from the podium.

"About time!" I murmured.

I was hoping that it was time to plant the tree, but, no, a man rose to speak. He was an odd-looking Josie—long, frizzy gray hair, goatee, potbelly, tinted granny glasses, tiedyed T-shirt, jeans, old sneakers. I was aghast that he was not better dressed for the occasion.

He introduced himself as Boom-boom Brogan. He was a disc jockey from what I gather was a popular local radio station, WBAZ-FM.

Who invited him to speak? I wondered. I was appalled at his lack of manners—why, he did not even remove his purple glasses when he addressed us.

That's the problem with civilization today, it is all going to— I caught myself.

No, I thought, *not all of civilization is going to rot. That is what I have learned from these four girls. They have shown me that everything isn't all bad, that some people do care.*

Finally, after what seemed like ages, it came time to plant the tree. Mrs. Sargent asked Sabrina, Connie, Daisy, and Megan to come over to the dogwood. She handed a shovel to Connie. Connie dug into the big mound of earth that was beside the hole and dropped some dirt on the tree's burlap root ball. Everyone clapped as she handed the shovel to Megan.

Megan placed a shovel of dirt into the hole.

Then it was Daisy's turn.

Then Sabrina's.

Then Mrs. Sargent took a turn. She invited everyone in the audience to come up and throw some dirt into the hole. A line quickly formed. Connie and the other girls, meanwhile, returned to their seats.

As I sat there, fanning myself, I noticed Megan elbow Connie and point to a branch on the dogwood tree. Connie opened her eyes wide. She excitedly nudged Sabrina, and then Sabrina nudged Daisy to take a look. All four girls gaped at the tree, and then they gaped at me.

I peered up at the tree. It was the strangest thing. A branch was jiggling up and down.

But how could it? There was no wind. There was not even a hint of a breeze. I glanced around. No one else seemed to notice the branch. Just the girls and me.

The really crazy thing was, it was as if the branch was waving to me, trying to get my attention! Then, as if that was not odd enough, a large bud suddenly appeared on the branch! I was sure I was seeing things. How could there be a bud? It wasn't spring! In a few weeks, trees would be dropping their leaves and we would be waking up to frost on the lawns.

Yet there it was, plain as day: a bud.

As I stared at the bud, it burst into a lovely white blossom!

I gasped. I turned and peered around. No one else was aware of the blossom. No one else but the girls and me. The four of them looked perfectly delighted. They knew why a bud on the tree had mysteriously blossomed.

And so did I.